14

[DOUBLE DETECTIVES]

The Tunnel
of Bones

by Zack Norris

D1115451

STERLING CHILDREN'S BOOKS
New York

For Meredith, who loves puns and palindromes
almost as much as Cody and Otis.

STERLING CHILDREN'S BOOKS
New York

An Imprint of Sterling Publishing
387 Park Avenue South
New York, NY 10016

ISBN 978-1-4027-9147-5

Distributed in Canada by Sterling Publishing
c/o Canadian Manda Group, 165 Dufferin Street
Toronto, Ontario, Canada M6K 3H6
Distributed in the United Kingdom by GMC Distribution Services
Castle Place, 166 High Street, Lewes, East Sussex, England BN7 1XU
Distributed in Australia by Capricorn Link (Australia) Pty. Ltd.
P.O. Box 704, Windsor, NSW 2756, Australia

For information about custom editions, special sales, and premium
and corporate purchases, please contact Sterling Special Sales
at 800-805-5489 or specialsales@sterlingpublishing.com.

Designed by Susan Gerber

Manufactured in the United States of America
Lot #:
2   4   6   8   10   9   7   5   3   1
08/12

www.sterlingpublishing.com/kids

[Chapter One]

The thief crept from the shadows and headed for the art gallery a few doors away. He was going to steal a painting for a very special customer. Breaking in was easy. He simply inserted the key into the shiny lock with his white-gloved hand, turned it, and stepped inside. He knew there would be no burglar alarm—in fact, he knew everything there was to know about the gallery.

He removed the painting from the wall and carefully hung a forgery in its place. The thief allowed himself a moment to admire the fake painting—it was expertly done. Before he left the gallery, he took a lock-picking tool from his pocket and placed it in the middle of the floor where it was sure to be seen. *Let them think a burglar picked the brand new* fool-proof *lock!* The thief laughed to himself.

Back in his room, he telephoned his connection.

The man on the other end of the call had been waiting—and he thought he had been waiting too long. "Hello?!" he snapped as he blinked his beady eyes.

"It's me," said the thief. "I have the package for your customer. You don't sound like you're in a good mood." He chuckled. "It was a piece of cake. I even left a hook pick behind so that idiot of a detective would think the burglar lost it."

"What did you do that for?" squealed the man. He was so angry that he slapped one of his tiny ears with a big paw of a hand. That hurt, and it made him even madder.

"I couldn't resist. This is so much fun!"

"Oh, shut up! I know this is a game to you, but the rest of us aren't playing. We're in it for the money, and if you keep fooling around with your stupid tricks, you're going to mess things up for all of us." He clenched his hand into a fist. "That wouldn't be good for you. If you pull another stunt like that, you won't be laughing."

The smile faded from the thief's face. He gripped the phone tightly. "Don't you threaten me. I'm the kingpin of this whole operation, not you. If you ever talk to me like that again, *you're* the one who won't be laughing. If you understand, say, '*Yes, sir.*'"

The man gulped when he heard those words. "Y-y-y-yes, sir. I was only j-j-joking," he stammered. His nervous, high-pitched laugh sounded like the bark of a hyena.

The thief smiled once more. "Good. I'm glad I cheered you up. Now I'll get back to planning our big job. It's going to be the most fun of all. The icing on the cake!"

[Chapter Two]

Cody Carson raced through the damp, dark tunnel, following the stream of light from the bulb on his miner's hat. If not for the hat, his brown hair would have been standing straight up with fear. He glanced sideways at his twin brother, Otis, running beside him, his eyes wide with fright.

They were being chased, and the *thud, thud, thud* of the feet hurrying behind them made their blood run cold. Whoever, or *whatever*, was chasing them was *rattling*. Suddenly, Cody tripped on something and crashed to the dirt floor of the tunnel. He found himself staring right into the empty eye sockets of a human skull.

"Get up!" Otis panted as he pulled Cody to his feet. "We've got to keep running!"

As they dashed through the twisting tunnel, both boys were sure their lungs were about to explode.

Then, with horror, they realized they could run no more. They had reached a dead end, piled with skulls and bones. They looked around frantically, eyes searching the shadows, but there was no way out. The rattling sound stopped just a few feet behind them.

"Turn around, boys," said a terrifying, hollow voice.

Trembling, Cody and Otis looked over their shoulders. A tall skeleton towered in the darkness, pointing a bony finger at them. "You are both in great danger," it said. Then the skull opened its mouth and cackled.

"Agghh!" Cody and Otis shrieked as they both sat bolt upright in their beds. They looked at each other and knew instantly that they'd had the same nightmare. This hadn't happened in a long time, but dreams were something the twins occasionally shared.

"Whew! It was just a dream!" said Cody, wiping the sweat from his forehead.

"Yeah, a dream that felt incredibly *real*," answered Otis. "What *was* that creepy place?"

"No idea. But we can't think about it now," said Cody, glancing at the alarm clock. "It's almost time to go to the airport!"

Both boys leaped out of bed, and in the rush of last-minute packing they forgot all about the nightmare and the warning it held.

[Chapter Three]

"I already love Paris!" said Cody Carson. His brown eyes danced as he ogled the dessert cart. "They all look so delicious. I don't know which one to pick!" He looked at his father. "Don't you think I should get two of them? After all, this IS the dessert capital of the universe."

Mr. Carson shook his head. "We'll be here for a week, Cody. You don't have to eat seven days' worth of pastry right now, and there will be lots of food at the party tonight, too."

"It's so hard to choose! I'm *dessert stressed*." Cody chuckled. He loved making up palindromes—words or phrases that read the same backward and forward— almost as much as he loved dessert.

"I guess you just don't know *where to tart*," Otis said with a grin, testing out a new pun. He pushed his shaggy brown hair out of his eyes and looked at his brother. "I know what you're going to say, so don't say it."

"No, don't say it!" their cousin Rae Lee chimed in. She was too late.

"*Sit on a potato pan, Otis!*" Cody said. It was his favorite palindrome, and he used it every chance he got.

"If I hear that one again, I think I'll go crazy," Rae said.

"If you fall in the river in Paris, you go *in Seine*," Otis told her.

"Cut it *out*, you guys!" Rae gave her short, dark hair a tug in frustration.

Cody grinned and opened his mouth to say something.

"*Non!*" Maxim Chatterton said quickly. "That means *no* in French, and I mean 'no' in every language. The next time you open your mouth I want you to be putting a piece of pastry into it." He rattled his newspaper, *Le Figaro*, and went back to reading about the recent crime wave in Paris. Maxim took great interest in crime stories, so the twins and Rae ended up knowing more than most kids about bank heists and ransom notes. Now that Mr. Carson was a world-famous painter, Maxim was very busy as his art agent, but ever since the twins' mother had passed away years ago, he had always made time to be an all-around helper and friend to the Carsons.

The doors of the bustling café were open to the street, and a warm breeze wafted inside. The sun was shining, and they could hear someone playing a tune on a violin somewhere nearby. It was the perfect day to be in Paris. They had just dropped off their luggage at the home of the twins' uncle, Detective Newton Andrews, who had invited them to stay for a week. He lived in a beautiful building not far from the Louvre Museum. His apartment took up the first two floors, and even had a little garden in the back. The Carsons, Rae, and Maxim were all looking forward to the big party he had planned that evening to welcome them.

"I asked your uncle to join us for lunch if he's able to take a break from work," Mr. Carson mentioned to the twins. "He hasn't seen you since you were very small."

Mr. Carson smiled, and he had a faraway look in his eyes for a moment. "Newton wanted to work for Scotland Yard since he was a kid. He was *obsessed* with the idea. Your mom and I didn't think he'd actually do it, but he did!"

"Wasn't it hard for an American detective to get hired at a famous police agency like Scotland Yard?" asked Cody.

"You don't have to be British to work there," explained Mr. Carson. "Anyone can apply for the job, as long as they've lived in the United Kingdom for three years and plan to live there permanently."

"Yeah, and Uncle Newton isn't just *any* American detective," added Otis. "Didn't you tell us he is one of the world's top experts on art theft?"

"Definitely. That's why he was invited to Paris to teach French detectives about it. But then this wave of art thefts began, and he was asked to stay to work on the case," said Mr. Carson. "Here comes your uncle now!"

A man with gray hair, a neatly trimmed mustache, and twinkling blue eyes greeted everyone as he approached the table. "Glad I could join you for lunch. It's been a long time," he said, shaking Mr. Carson's hand warmly. Then he turned to Rae and the twins. "You're practically grown up now. My sister would have been so proud to see how you three turned out."

"I recognize you from Mom's photo album, Uncle Newton," said Otis softly. "She had blue eyes just like yours."

"That's true. I miss her, and I know you do, too," said the detective, resting a hand on Otis's shoulder. "So glad that all of you could come for a visit."

"So are we," said Cody. "Paris is amazing!" He was still eyeing the pastries, trying to decide which to eat first, when Jules, the owner of the café, stopped by their table. He was tall, with green eyes and blond hair. He was wearing a dark suit and a shiny blue tie.

"*Bonjour*," he greeted Detective Andrews.

"*Bonjour*, Jules. This is my brother-in-law from America, Hayden Carson, his twin boys, Cody and Otis, their cousin Rae, and Hayden's friend and agent, Maxim Chatterton. Maxim speaks French fluently, but the others are still learning. You know my French is still pretty bad." He turned to the group. "Luckily, I never have trouble ordering food here because Jules speaks perfect English," he said.

"Thank you, Detective. My mother was American. I'm used to speaking English to you." Jules looked around the table. "Did Detective Andrews tell you how we met? A couple of months ago, he came in and arrested my top chef in the middle of the dinner rush! It turned out that he was a small-time art thief." He chuckled and shook his head.

"I can laugh about it now, but business was terrible for a while, and I nearly had to close my café. Fortunately, I found a new chef who is working out well. In fact, he is making the food for your party right now."

"After the arrest, Jules and I became friends," explained Detective Andrews. "That's why I asked if his restaurant would cater the party. You're joining us tonight, aren't you, Jules?"

"Of course!" Jules said. "I wouldn't dream of missing it."

Jules noticed that Cody was staring at the pastries on the dessert cart. "Now here's a young man who appreciates dessert! Let me tell you about the pastries. That one is a *tarte tatin*, a small caramel apple pie. And these colorful little cakes are called *petits fours*. Let's pick several for the table, and you can all share. That way you'll get a taste of everything."

Soon the table was covered with chocolate cakes, puffs of pastry and whipped cream, custards, and cookies.

"Do you have a moment to join us, Jules?" asked Maxim as he folded his newspaper. "I've been reading about the art thefts here in Paris for several months."

"Oh, yes." Jules nodded, pulling up a chair. "It's terrible. The thief is very skilled. Most of the time, the gallery owners don't even know that a break-in has happened. You see, it appears at first as though nothing is missing. The thief replaces stolen paintings with excellent forgeries—fakes that look exactly like the original art. Sometimes the theft isn't discovered until the thief publishes a note in the newspaper."

Detective Andrews was scowling. "Yes, this thief thinks he's very funny, but he isn't."

Mr. Carson shook his head. "This is like déjà vu. When I had my first show in Paris years ago, there was a similar wave of art thefts. I was lucky that my paintings were not stolen."

Jules nodded gravely. "Yes, you were very lucky. Most stolen paintings are never recovered. They are sold again and again until no one can prove who really owns them anymore. Criminals are selling to greedy, rich collectors who will do anything to get their hands on what they want—and who don't care how a piece of art was obtained or how much they have to pay. No doubt about it, there is a lot of money to be made on the black market for art. Everyone in Paris is upset about these thefts."

Mr. Carson began to speak, but he was interrupted by the sound of breaking glass. A man's voice called out in French.

"That didn't sound very far away," said Rae as she jumped from her chair. The twins were already heading for the door.

"Come on, let's see what's up!" cried Otis.

Jules, Maxim, and Mr. Carson followed. Detective Andrews was already on his cell phone, calling for backup.

They hurried past the shoe repair shop next door to the café and found a man standing outside a small art gallery called Claude's Fine Art. He was shaking his fist and shouting at some boys who were running down the street. The window was smashed, and the sidewalk in front of the gallery was littered with broken glass. A couple of rocks lay in the middle of the mess.

"C'mon! Let's try to catch them!" shouted Rae.

Rae and the twins were fast runners, but the older boys had a head start. One of them wore a green sweatshirt; the other two wore black hoodies. Otis was in the lead. "Turn left!" he huffed as the boys rounded a corner.

Cody and Rae followed Otis down a cobblestone street. The boy in the green sweatshirt looked over his shoulder and shouted something to the others. Rae and the twins were gaining on the boys when the three made another quick turn. Otis led the way around the corner and then came to a halt. Cody and Rae pulled up behind him. They were all panting.

"Where'd they go?" Cody asked, scratching his head.

Otis put his hands on his knees and took some deep breaths. "I don't know," he said. "It's like they just vanished into thin air. Poof! Gone."

[Chapter Four]

"**I**'m sorry we didn't catch those guys, Uncle Newton," said Otis later that afternoon.

"Don't apologize. It's a *good* thing you didn't catch them," answered Detective Andrews. "They might have been a gang of street thugs, and you could have gotten hurt."

"It's possible," Otis said thoughtfully. "Our sensei, that's our karate master, tells us to avoid fighting. But those guys broke a window. We didn't want them to get away with it."

Rae and Cody nodded.

They were all enjoying the party that Detective Andrews had arranged in their honor. A little later in the evening, the detective planned to unveil a picture that Mr. Carson had painted for him. It was sitting on an easel in a corner of the living room, draped with a cloth.

"I'm just glad you three are all right," said the detective. "A couple of other gallery owners have had their windows broken in the past few months. It seems that these vandals just like to break things. The gallery owners have enough trouble with all the robberies going on."

Mr. Carson wandered over. "How are the investigations going?"

The detective frowned. "Not very well. I am working with a new director, Monsieur Anton Brun. He has different ideas than the old director did. He thinks that the theft of art is not very important. He wants all the police to spend time chasing down bank robbers and car thieves and the like. Oh, he *says* he wants the art theft cases solved, but he keeps assigning members of the force to other cases." His face pinched with worry.

Maxim joined the group. "I heard what you were saying, Detective. It sounds as if the new director is making some very poor choices. I can't imagine anyone in law enforcement making light of art theft anywhere. In the city of Paris, known for its many masterpieces, that behavior is just unbelievable. Billions of dollars' worth of art are stolen every year, isn't that right?"

The detective nodded. "Art is often easy to steal. Big

museums like the Louvre can afford many guards and state-of-the-art security systems like motion detectors and heat sensors. Smaller museums can't afford such high-tech security. Many small galleries don't even have burglar alarms."

Rae and the twins exchanged glances. They had been hanging on the detective's every word. They all loved mysteries, and gadgets like motion detectors and heat sensors really got them interested. Maxim glanced at them and groaned. "Don't get any ideas, you three," he said. "We're here to enjoy Paris. Leave the sleuthing to Detective Andrews and the police."

"Yes, it's about time we had a real vacation without you all chasing crooks around," said Mr. Carson, putting an arm around his two boys and raising an eyebrow at his niece.

The three nodded. "Sure, Dad," said Cody. He crossed his fingers behind his back.

"I think that even *I* should stop thinking about work right now," said the detective. "After all, this is a party. I want you to meet some of my friends." He gestured to a man standing by the window. "Martin, allow me to introduce my American guests," he called.

A man with wavy hair, wearing a sweater and perfectly creased pants, walked over. On the way, he paused, frowned, and bent down to brush some dust off the toe of one of his shiny brown leather shoes with a napkin. He looked a little embarrassed as he stood up. "Hello, I am Martin Durand, an old friend of the detective." He smiled warmly at the group. "You must be Mr. Carson," he said, turning to the twins' father. "I am very excited about seeing your painting tonight. I know your work well."

"So do I," said a tall young man who appeared by Detective Andrews's side. His straight brown hair fell over his collar. "My name is Marcel Remy. I am a student at the Académie des Arts. A struggling student of the starving-artist type, I might add. By the way, the food is wonderful," he said to the detective.

"*Merci, mon ami.* Jules, the owner of Chez Jules brought it over earlier. There he is now! Over here, Jules," he called. When Jules approached, the detective introduced everyone.

"Marcel may be poor now, but I know he won't be for long. He is as talented with paint as Jules is with food!" Detective Andrews told them. "A few of Marcel's teachers are here, and they are all bragging about the quality of his work. Marcel, I want you to meet my brother-in-law." The detective turned to his guest of honor. "Perhaps you might give Marcel some advice on getting agents and shows?"

"Of course!" said Mr. Carson. "I know several

people here in Paris who are looking for gifted young artists."

"Wonderful!" said the detective, clapping Mr. Carson on the shoulder. "And Martin Durand is definitely someone you should both know here in the Paris art world. He framed most of the art in my home," said the detective. "Monsieur Durand is so skilled that when I'm in England I send art to him for framing. You can see that I've kept him busy. I love these pictures so much that I take them with me whenever I'll be away from London for an extended stay."

"That's a lot of pictures," Otis observed, smiling. "Your walls are *covered*, and you're *undercover!*"

"I'm not really an undercover detective, Otis," said Detective Andrews with a smile.

"It's a pretty good pun, though." Monsieur Durand chuckled. "By the way, I have an interesting story to tell you," he said to the twins. "I owe a great deal to your uncle here. He changed my life, you know. I was a—"

Detective Andrews held up a hand for silence. "You don't have to tell," he said. "The past is the past."

Monsieur Durand smiled. "But it's my pleasure," he insisted. "I'm so happy about the way things turned out." He turned back to the twins, Maxim, and Mr. Carson. "You'll be surprised to know that years ago Detective Andrews arrested me in London."

Everyone stood very still. Monsieur Durand looked around at them all. "That's right, I was a criminal—an art thief. Detective Andrews was put on the case, and not long after that happened I found myself in the back of what you Americans call a paddy wagon on the way to jail."

Maxim gasped. "Good heavens!"

Otis was coming up with so many puns in his head that he had to bite his lip to keep from saying them out loud: *Did he get to use a* cell *phone? Prison walls aren't* built to scale. *Maybe he was* framed!

"Being in jail gave me lots of time to think," Monsieur Durand continued. "I realized how wrong I had been. The first thing I did when I got out of jail was visit Detective Andrews and thank him. If not for him, I probably would have remained a common criminal like the disgusting thieves who are robbing galleries and museums right now. Instead, I learned everything I could about framing all kinds of artwork—paintings, posters, photographs, and so on. There is a lot more to learn than you'd think! I have worked hard to become a respected member of society." He set his lips in an angry line. "If I can help bring these lowlife criminals to justice, I will."

"Monsieur Durand doesn't keep his past a secret," Marcel Remy told the Carson bunch. "He even came to my school to speak about his success story. It's an inspiration to kids to steer clear of a life of crime."

"I couldn't be prouder of your accomplishments, Martin," said Detective Andrews, smiling at Monsieur Durand. "And now I think it's about time to unveil the painting and toast our guests of honor." Andrews clapped his hands. "Attention! Attention, everyone! This is the moment we have all been waiting for. I am going to unveil an original painting by my brother-in-law, Hayden Carson. He knows that I love seeing birds in flight, so he has created a picture of them especially for me." The detective stepped closer to the painting covered up on the easel. "And now," he began, but stopped suddenly. The lights had begun to flicker.

While everyone was paying attention to the lights, they heard a horrible wailing and screeching. The party guests began jumping out of the way as several furry creatures brushed past their legs. A few people cried out in alarm.

"Look!" Rae nudged Otis.

"It's okay, everyone! Don't be afraid," Otis said loudly. Nobody paid any attention, for just then the lights went out completely, and the room was plunged into darkness.

[Chapter Five]

For the next several minutes there was chaos and confusion in the room. Then suddenly the lights snapped back on. "Where did all these cats come from?" someone shouted.

Five cats were wandering around the room. One was on the table where trays of food were laid out for the guests. It was standing in the middle of a cheese platter. Another cat was batting a pastry across the carpet, and another was watching, its back arched high in the air. The other two cats were chasing each other across a velvet sofa.

"*Achoo!*" A woman with blond hair pulled up into an enormous beehive sneezed. "Why didn't you tell me about these animals, Detective Andrews?" she asked crossly. "You know I'm allergic!"

"I'm so sorry, madame," the detective said hurriedly. "I don't know where they came from. I don't have any cats!"

"Someone wanted you to have some," Rae announced. She pulled a curtain aside to reveal a large cat carrier with an open door.

Monsieur Durand glared at a cat that crossed his path. "One of those creatures clawed my shoe," he grumbled. "I just bought these shoes in Italy, and they were very expensive! I'll have to take them to Lamont's for repair. That's the finest shoe repair shop in Paris, and right in the neighborhood, in case you need one while you're here," he said to Mr. Carson.

The sneezing woman let out a shriek. "There's cat hair all over my dress!"

"Please calm down, madame," pleaded Detective Andrews.

Otis crossed his arms. "I think I noticed the circuit-breaker box over here," he said, walking into the hallway. "The cover is open. Someone used the confusion created by the cats as an opportunity to flip the main breaker switch and cut the electricity. When they finished whatever they were up to, they switched the lights back on."

Marcel was hurrying around the room scooping up cats. Otis helped him get them all back into the carrier. The last one didn't want to be caught, and Otis had to dive under a sofa to get it. He gently pushed the cat inside the carrier and latched the door. "Whew!"

Rae bent down and examined the carrier. "It looks like there is some kind of sensor thingie here on the front," she said, pointing to a small black square.

"Hey—look what I found on the floor behind the sofa!" said Cody. He held up a tiny remote control. "Somebody had this planned out way in advance." He pointed the remote at the cat carrier and pressed a green button.

"No, no, no!" cried Detective Andrews. It was too late. The cats came bounding out of the carrier into the room. Marcel, Rae, and the twins hurried to gather them again, but one of the cats leaped onto a table holding a vase full of flowers. The vase crashed to the floor and rolled a few feet, knocking over the easel that held Mr. Carson's painting.

The cloth that had been covering the painting fell to the floor, revealing an empty easel. "The painting is gone!" Detective Andrews gasped in dismay. "It's been stolen!"

A note was pinned to the easel. The detective read it aloud first in French, and then in English:

I guess you were taking a catnap.

Detective Andrews's face turned red. "Another one of these infuriating messages!" he fumed. "I'm so sorry about this, my dear friends," he said to his guests. "What a party this turned out to be!" He looked around the room. "The thief could still be here."

The guests glanced at each other nervously.

Rae had slipped out of the room and was checking for clues. "I think the thief is gone!" she called out. "I found this by the door." She came back into the room carrying Mr. Carson's bird painting. She held it carefully by one corner, using a paper cocktail napkin to avoid getting fingerprints on the frame. In her other hand she held a cat toy shaped like a fuzzy mouse. It had another note pinned to its tail. She handed the note to Detective Andrews:

Good-bye for now. I am enjoying our game of cat and mouse.

The detective wrinkled his nose. "Someone has a sense of humor that stinks," he said. He leaned the painting carefully against the wall and tucked the note into the pocket of his pants. "I will have to take this painting to my office immediately. The police will dust for fingerprints, though they have rarely found any on stolen art in the past."

"That thief is pretty clever," said Otis quietly to Cody and Rae. "He laid out the whole plan ahead of time and hid among the guests to pull it off."

"The thief *could* be a *she*," said Rae.

"The thief could even have been one of the invited guests," said Cody. He had barely finished his sentence when the lights went out again. There was a scuffling commotion coming from the stairs. "Help! Help! Someone stop him!" a man called out.

Two figures raced through the dark room, knocking into the guests. "Stop!" Cody yelled, as someone rushed past him. Cody tackled the figure and held on tight. "Let me go!" a man's voice called out. Then another voice shouted, "Hold onto him! I'll get rope to tie him up!" A door slammed.

When the lights went on a moment later, Cody was holding onto Detective Andrews's ankle. "I just realized that voice was yours, Uncle Newton. I was going to let go," Cody told him sheepishly.

"I found the circuit-breaker box and turned the lights back on," Marcel said breathlessly. "What happened?"

Detective Andrews didn't pay any attention to Marcel. He was staring at the easel, which was no longer empty. "Look!" He pointed to the painting that was now on the easel. It was a picture of a large cat holding an even bigger bird in its mouth by the tail. The two creatures were eyeballing each other. The bird looked fiercely at the cat, whose eyes were wide with fright.

"Very funny," said the detective grimly. "*This* is one of the missing gallery paintings!"

Martin Durand looked pale. "That's *Scaredy-Cat* by that new artist who's become such a star." He snapped his fingers. "Her name is Kitty Lyons. I've framed several of her pieces for gallery owners."

"I met her last week at an opening," said a man in a black beret. "She's a mousy little thing."

The detective gave him a grim look. "Isn't it enough that the thief is making jokes? This is very serious." He let out a long sigh. "Somehow the thief was able to put the painting here before he ran out the door." He looked at Mr. Carson. "And I'm sorry to say that he got away with your marvelous painting. I will do everything in my power to get it back. For now, I am at least grateful to have recovered one of the other stolen pieces. I wonder why the thief left it here."

"Because it's a forgery," Marcel said quickly. "I can tell even from a distance."

"It's a fake? How do you know?" Detective Andrews asked.

Marcel's face reddened as everyone in the room turned to look at him. "Let me show you," he said.

As Marcel made his way through the crowd, Mr. Carson bent down in front of the painting and looked at it closely. "I haven't seen this particular painting before, but it certainly looks like Kitty Lyons's work to me," he said. "She always paints a tiny cat with its tail curled over its back beside her signature, like this one." He pointed out the small detail.

Marcel stepped up beside him. "That's right," he said, "but I've studied *Scaredy-Cat* in one of my classes. The brush strokes on the tail are going in the wrong direction here. Plus, the cat's eyes are a little crossed."

"Interesting," said Mr. Carson. "You are very observant!"

"This painting is definitely a forgery, Detective Andrews," said Marcel. "I'm afraid the thief was playing another joke on you."

The detective was quiet for a moment. "Well, I'll have the last laugh." He looked around at the guests. "I'm not going to let him spoil the party. Please, everyone, go ahead and enjoy yourselves. I have to go to my office for a while. If I have not returned by midnight, my housekeeper will lock up." He nodded to the crowd and left.

"Too bad the detective had to leave," Marcel remarked.

"Yeah," Cody agreed. "And I know Dad must be really upset that his new painting has been stolen." He sighed. "Are you studying to be a painter, like my dad?"

"I hope so," Marcel answered. "Right now I'm just

studying and trying to pay the bills. It's not easy in an expensive city like Paris."

The two of them talked for a while. Marcel told Cody how he got interested in painting when he was Cody's age. "I had been drawing and coloring with pencils for years. One day my father bought me a set of oil paints and some small canvases. Once I began painting, no one could keep me away from it. I painted almost every day." He nodded toward Otis and Rae. "How do you three spend your days?"

Cody's mouth was off and running. "When we're home in Deerville, New York, we go to Deerville Day School. That isn't very often, because we travel a lot with Dad. When we're on the road, Maxim gives us our lessons. There are lots of things we like to do. We know how to pilot planes and drive cars, and we all have black belts in karate." He smiled as he looked sideways at Marcel. "We know how to pick locks, too."

"Really?" Marcel chuckled. "I'm afraid my life isn't half as interesting as yours has been. As a boy, the closest I got to adventure was exploring the city with my dog, Stephan. He was a little brown mutt, but so smart. What a good friend! Do you have a dog?"

"Yeah, he's a golden Labrador named Dude. He's pretty funny, but probably not as smart as your dog was. Our parrot, Pauley, drives him crazy by telling him to sit or roll over. Dude falls for it almost every time!" Marcel laughed along with Cody.

"I'll tell you something else." Cody's eyes danced. "I tried to teach Pauley some French, but it didn't exactly work out. He just keeps saying, '*Pauley vous francais?*'! I don't think Otis and Rae are too happy about hearing that over and over a thousand times a day."

Marcel grinned. "You guys are *fantastique!*" Then he glanced at his watch. "It's getting late," he said. "I'm meeting some people in the catacombs tonight—perhaps you three would like to come with me sometime and experience a part of Paris that tourists never get to see?" he asked with a mysterious smile.

"What are the catacombs?" asked Cody, instantly interested.

While Otis and Rae were busy talking to Martin Durand about his life as a thief, Marcel told Cody all about the Paris catacombs. "There are thousands of tunnels under Paris," he explained. "There are bank vaults and galleries and nightclubs hidden away. Of course, the Paris metro trains run underground, and the sewer is there, too. But my favorite parts of the catacombs are the old limestone quarries. There is a giant maze of them underground."

"Sounds spooky," said Cody.

"It is," said Marcel. "But it's also really fun. People

have been having parties there for years. My friends and I go down there and play music, dance, paint on the walls, even swim in the underground pools. The really spooky part though ... is the bones. In the eighteenth and nineteenth centuries, skeletons were taken out of overcrowded cemeteries and stored down there. Imagine stacks and stacks of skulls and bones."

Cody felt a shiver of recognition as he remembered his nightmare. "I had a dream about something like that last night," he said. "Isn't that weird?"

Marcel chuckled. "Maybe you read about the catacombs in a Paris guidebook before you went to sleep."

Cody looked doubtful. "Maybe. I can't remember. Can anybody go down there?"

"Well, no, not where we go. It's actually off-limits. But there are guided tours of the parts that are open to the public."

Cody could hardly wait to tell his brother and Rae. He didn't want to go on a guided tour, though. What he really wanted to do was explore the quarry tunnels with Marcel and his friends.

"You asked if we would like to come with you sometime. Did you mean it?" Cody asked as Detective Andrews's party guests were starting to leave.

"Sure," said Marcel. "There's an underground party

planned for tomorrow night. Call me tomorrow if you want to come." He scribbled his phone number on a piece of paper and handed it to Cody. "I'm going to say good-bye to your dad," he said. "See you soon!"

"I can't wait to see the catacombs!" Cody called after him. "And I know Rae and Otis will be just as excited." He glanced at the number and put it in his pocket. Then he noticed a piece of torn newspaper lying on the floor. He picked it up, and the number on it caught his eye. There was something familiar about it. He took out the slip of paper Marcel had just given him. Sure enough, the numbers matched!

He read the words above the number and tried to remember if he'd learned them in his French lessons. He went over each one slowly. Pretty soon he had figured out enough to know that they were part of an advertisement:

`Perfect copies of master paintings for sale . . . 32 rue des Fleurs, #2B . . . Prices are reasonable!`

It's like advertising that you can create a forgery, Cody thought. He looked for Marcel, but he had already left.

[Chapter Six]

That evening, Cody told Otis and Rae about the catacombs and the adventure that was planned for the following night. Otis bounced up and down on his bed. "Yes!" he cried, pumping his fist in the air. "This trip just keeps getting better and better!"

"I'm surprised you went for it so fast, Cody," Rae said.

Cody looked at her and crossed his arms. "What's that supposed to mean?"

"Don't look at me like that," said Rae. "You know that even though you've got a big mouth, you're usually kind of . . . careful."

Cody's mouth dropped open. "You make it sound like I'm a wimp. I just like to think things through."

"Chill out." Otis reached over and tapped him on the arm. "That's all Rae means. Usually you'll consider all the angles before you decide to do something."

"It's smart to do that," he said, a little too defensively. He took a breath. "But who could resist an offer to explore hidden tunnels under Paris? Besides, I really like Marcel, and I felt right away that we could trust him." He pulled Marcel's phone number and the piece of newspaper from his pocket. "Look at this, though. Kind of weird, huh?" He translated for them the words he'd figured out.

"You've got the words right," Rae said after she examined the ad. "Uh-huh," Otis agreed. Then they saw that the number in the ad was the same as Marcel's. "Definitely weird," Rae said. "But it could seem strange to us because of all the art thefts and what happened at the party. Otherwise we might not think anything of it. I mean, your dad has told us how part of his homework was copying great master paintings when he was in art school."

"Yeah," said Cody. "He did it to learn the styles of the master painters. Besides, people hang prints of their favorite paintings on their walls. You can even buy kits to paint copies of pictures. Why *not* own a painting that looks a lot like the real thing? It isn't illegal."

Rae traced a pattern on the bedspread with her finger. "That's true," she said, "but it's something to think about." She opened her eyes wide. "What if

Marcel knew the cat painting was a forgery because *he* painted it? Even your dad couldn't tell it was a fake."

"Right," said Otis, sitting up straighter. "And maybe, just maybe, Marcel was the one who brought it to the party. We couldn't see where he was when the lights went out."

"The second time the lights went out, he was the one who fixed the circuit breaker and switched them back on, so he knew where the breaker box was. Maybe he was the one who turned them off, too," added Rae.

Otis was nodding. Cody, however, was shaking his head. "*You* found the circuit breaker the first time, Otis. Marcel could have heard you say that you saw it in the hallway. Or maybe he just saw it there, too. Anyway, it wasn't that hard to find. Nothing proves he brought the cat painting to the party or that he was the one who painted it."

Rae stood up. "You're right. What would help is if we knew whether Marcel wrote his number on the same kind of paper as was used in the notes. We could see if the handwriting is similar, too."

Cody held up his hand. "Hold on. How would we do that? Uncle Newton took the notes."

"Duh," said Otis. "He might still have them in his pants pocket. We could find out."

Cody got up and stood in front of the door. "Wait a minute. That means we'd have to sneak into his room while he's sleeping and start searching around. He could wake up, and we'd get in trouble. Besides, how would we know where to look?"

"You know how Dad always puts his pants on the chair in his room when he goes to sleep? Maybe Uncle Newton does, too," suggested Otis.

Cody tapped his foot. "No way. This doesn't sound good. What are we going to say if we get caught?"

Rae and Otis exchanged glances. "We don't all have to go," said Rae. "I'll do it. I can be really quiet. If he wakes up I'll just say I was sleepwalking!" She laughed.

"Out of the way, Cody," Otis said. "Remember, we're trying to help Uncle Newton. This case is upsetting him."

"Okay, okay," Cody said. He moved aside to let Rae pass. "But be really careful."

"Wish me luck," Rae whispered as she left. She tiptoed barefoot down the hall past her empty room and the room where Mr. Carson was sleeping. Earlier, she had seen the detective enter the room at the end of the hall, and now she could hear him snoring. The door was open an inch and she held her breath as she opened it wider little by little, praying that it didn't squeak.

Otis had been right. In the light from the hallway she saw a pair of pants folded neatly over a chair by the door. Cautiously she found one of the pockets, her fingers feeling for the crisp paper she had felt when she'd handed the detective the second note. There was a folded handkerchief in the pocket but nothing else.

She picked up the pants to go through the other pocket. Just then the detective let out a tremendous *snort*! Rae jumped back in fright and bumped into the dresser. She heard something rattle as it fell to the floor. The detective snorted again and turned over. Rae waited, sweat breaking out on her forehead.

When the detective went back to snoring and remained still, she picked up the pants again. As she went through the second pocket, she found the two notes. She withdrew them slowly, careful not to crinkle them. Then she tiptoed out and closed the door partway behind her.

"That was a close one," she whispered, back in the twins' room. "I found the notes." She opened them and smoothed them out on one of the bedspreads. Cody put the phone number beside them.

"No doubt about it. The paper is the same." He sighed.

"I can't tell about the handwriting, though," said Otis. "The notes and the number are kind of scribbled, and there are no letters to compare. The handwriting might be from the same person, or it might not."

"There are lots of notepads with the same paper, I bet," said Cody. "I don't think this tells us anything much. I like Marcel, and I don't think he's a criminal. You guys didn't talk to him as much as I did."

"I know," said Otis. "But we can't rule him out. We'll all have to keep an eye on him."

Rae picked up the notes. "Now I've got to put these back in the detective's pockets." She crossed her fingers as she left.

This time the detective wasn't snoring. He was perfectly still as she gently placed both notes back in the pocket of his pants. Then, as she was tiptoeing out the door, he suddenly sat bolt upright in bed. "Who's there? What are you doing in here?" he snapped.

Rae gulped. She turned slowly and looked at him. "Huh?" She rubbed her eyes and tried to sound confused. "I guess I got mixed up. I don't know how I got here. I must have been sleepwalking!"

[Chapter Seven]

"I didn't know you were a sleepwalker, Rae," Maxim said the next morning as they all walked to the Tuileries Gardens. "It never happened at the Carsons' house."

Rae stuffed her hands into her pockets. "I hope it never happens again," she said, looking at the ground. "I think I scared the poor detective."

"I'm sure he's had worse scares before." Maxim chuckled.

The Tuileries was a big park created in 1559. Maxim had told them all about it. The park was redesigned in 1664 by the same gardener who had designed the gardens at Versailles, the grand palace where many kings and queens had lived, including Marie Antoinette.

They all strolled around the park, admiring the flowers, the fountains with their crystal sprays of water, and the beautiful sculptures. There was a carousel in one corner of the park, and they all watched the little kids riding the colorful horses.

"Do you know that from inside these gardens you can see the Musée d'Orsay, the Arc de Triomphe, the Louvre, and the Eiffel Tower? There's a lot to see in Paris, and we should get started," said Mr. Carson.

"Let's check out the Eiffel Tower first!" said Cody, pointing to it rising majestically in the sky.

"Fine," Mr. Carson agreed. "Let's go! The view from the top is fabulous!"

He was right. When they got off the rattly elevator, everyone was thrilled to see the whole of Paris spread out before them. The Seine River snaked through the city. The wide, busy boulevards stretched out from the Arc de Triomphe like the spokes of a wheel. Rae snapped photo after photo with her smartphone.

After the visit to the Eiffel Tower, they dined in a café near the river, filling up on thin French pancakes called crêpes, with ham and melted cheese rolled up inside.

"What's for dessert?" Cody asked as soon as he'd finished his crêpe.

Mr. Carson laughed and put a hand on his stomach. "Nothing for me, I'm afraid," he said.

"Not for me either," said Maxim. "I'm stuffed."

"We have those errands to run, Maxim," said Mr. Carson. The way he looked at him made the twins curious.

"What kind of errands?" asked Otis.

"Oh, nothing that would interest you," said Mr. Carson quickly. "I'll bet Cody would be interested in dessert at Chez Jules, though."

"I think we all could go for that," said Otis.

"I'm thinking of a tarte tatin right now," said Rae. "On second thought, a chocolate éclair might be better. Can we really go there for dessert?"

"Why not? This is Paris, after all." Mr. Carson reached into his pocket and handed them each some money. He glanced at his watch. "It's later than I thought. I'll tell you what. We could all meet in an hour and a half in front of the Centre Pompidou— that's the museum of modern art with all the bright colors on the outside, remember? Of course, we could go on a guided tour of the catacombs if you'd prefer."

Rae and the twins looked at each other. Mr. Carson had never mentioned the catacombs before. "Let's go to the museum, Dad," said Cody. "I know you want to go, and we can see the catacombs another time."

"That's very thoughtful, Cody," said Mr. Carson. "Do you all know how to get around?"

Rae and the twins took their guidebooks out of their backpacks. "We've got maps, and we can get directions on our cell phones, Dad," said Cody. "We'll be fine." He was already edging away, thinking about which dessert he wanted. Mr. Carson nodded and then he and Maxim hurried to one of the bridges spanning the Seine River.

Soon, Rae and the twins were sitting happily at Chez Jules, digging into cream puffs and tarts. "I don't think I can leave this behind," Cody said. "It's all too delicious."

Jules stopped by the table to say hello.

"Put that away," he said with a smile when Rae took out her money. "On this holiday, the desserts are on me."

"That was pretty nice of him," Cody said, when Jules had left. "Do you think Dad and Maxim would come back for dinner tonight?"

"I think there might be at least *one* other restaurant in Paris they'd like to try," said Otis. "I'll bet other places have good pastries, too. While we're here, why don't we check on that gallery owner whose window got broken?"

They walked to the nearby gallery and noticed that a new plate-glass window had been installed. Peering through the glass, they could see the gallery owner sitting behind a desk. He looked exhausted and depressed.

"*Bonjour, monsieur,*" said Cody as they stepped

inside. "We were here yesterday when those boys broke your window. We ran after them, but we couldn't catch them."

The owner stood up and shook hands with each of them. "I'm Claude," he said. "You are good kids—not like those other guys. I've seen them around before, and I had a feeling they were up to no good. My son and I stayed in front of the store all night guarding the pictures. I had the new glass put in this morning. It was so expensive! The Argent company charges—how do you say in America? An arm and a leg?—but all the gallery owners use Argent because they're the best and they always get the job done quickly. Between the vandals and the robberies, we're all losing money." He waved his hand in disgust. "It's not just the money," he continued. "It's the idea that someone would steal these beautiful pictures. Who knows where they go? Who knows what happens to them? It makes me sick. Thank goodness none of mine have been taken. There are some very good ones here. Please feel free to take a look around."

"I like these pirate paintings," said Cody.

"That's one of the new artists," said Claude. "Cleve Reeves always paints pirates. I've also got a few pieces by that other new artist, Kitty Lyons."

"She's good. Do you think that's her real name?" Cody asked Otis.

"You've *gotta be kitten me*," joked Otis. "Seriously, I guess it could be. What were her parents thinking?"

He stepped in front of the Kitty Lyons painting, and his brother and Rae followed. It was a picture of two cats dancing.

"See, the brush strokes on the tails are going the way Marcel said they should," Rae observed.

"And the cats don't have crossed eyes," said Cody.

"It looks like a real Kitty Lyons all right," said Otis. "The little cat beside the signature is really, really tiny though." He got close to the picture and squinted. "Uh-oh. The cat's tail isn't curled over its body. It's going the wrong way!"

Rae and Cody examined the little cat.

"You're right," Rae said.

"Claude, we think this picture is a forgery," said Cody.

Claude rushed over. "Oh, *non, non, non*! I assure you that this is an authentic Kitty Lyons."

"I don't think so, monsieur," Otis said. "You see, our father is the painter Hayden Carson. Just last night he said that the cat beside the signature in a real Kitty Lyons painting always has its tail curled over its back."

43

Claude stroked his chin. "That's absolutely right," he said. He bent to examine the signature. Then he straightened up and said, "*Quelle horreur*! This painting *is* a forgery!" Claude wiped a hand over his brow. "This is horrible. The real painting was here this morning. I look at all the paintings every day as soon as I come in."

Cody had been walking around the gallery to see what else he could find. "Look at this, Claude," he said. "Somebody put tape over the lock. When you thought the place was locked up tight, somebody just walked right in. They took the real painting and replaced it with the forgery."

Claude saw the tape over the lock and put a hand to his mouth. "*Non*! Who could have done it? There have been so many customers coming in and out."

"Did you leave the shop today?" Cody asked.

"Yes, yes, of course I did. Every day for the past twenty years I have closed up for lunch at one o'clock and come back at two-thirty. I go to the café Chez Jules since it is so close to my gallery. But I always turn on the alarm when I close up the shop."

"Could you have forgotten today?"

Claude stood up straighter. "*Non*! Claude has never forgotten to turn on the alarm in twenty years!" He frowned. "Maybe there is something wrong with the alarm!" He went into a room at the back of the shop. When he came out, he was wringing his hands. "Someone has tampered with the system!"

"Probably the same person who put the tape over the lock," said Otis gravely.

"I'll put this in the back to show the police," said Claude as he put on a pair of special gloves. His shoulders sagged as he took the picture off the wall and carried it to the storeroom at the back of the gallery.

"Uh-oh," said Rae, pointing to a note stuck to the wall where the painting had been. "It's in French, but even I understand this one." She read it aloud:

Bonjour, Andrews! Surprise!

[Chapter Eight]

Claude called the police. A few minutes later, Detective Andrews arrived with an officer in uniform. Rae and the twins thought the detective looked a little worn out. Even his mustache drooped.

Detective Andrews examined the lock on the door while the officer wrapped the painting in plastic and put it in the trunk of the police car. While the detective was questioning Claude, he got a phone call from the director. Rae and the twins heard what sounded like an argument. The phone call ended with Detective Andrews stamping his foot, waving his arms around, and then getting into his car and driving away without even saying good-bye.

"I guess the director wanted him to go someplace else," said Cody.

"I heard the detective say that this investigation was more important than a stolen cameo brooch," Claude said indignantly.

"It's strange that the director of police doesn't think art theft is a top priority," Otis said. "I'm sorry, Claude."

Rae and Cody said that they were sorry, too. They said *au revoir* to Claude and began walking toward the modern art museum.

"Look! It's Martin Durand, from the party!" said Rae. "Let's say hello." She hurried toward Monsieur Durand.

"Hold up, Rae," Otis called to her. "Maybe we shouldn't let Monsieur Durand know that we've seen him. Look who he's talking to."

"Who is it?" asked Rae. Then she said, "Oh."

Cody stopped to study the man with Monsieur Durand. His jaw dropped. "It's Manny the Mole! He just got out of prison a little while ago."

Maxim's interest in crime stories kept Rae and the twins up to date on all the crooks. He had often talked about the American mobster called Manny the Mole—also called Manny Ha-Ha because of his strange, hyena-like laugh. Manny was a check forger, counterfeiter, and bank robber with ties to organized crime in New York City. His favorite bank-heist method was tunneling into vaults.

"It looks like his nickname doesn't come only from his tunneling," Otis said. "He kind of looks like a mole, with those short, stubby legs and big hands like a mole's paws."

Rae tilted her head to one side. "You know, I think you're right," she said. "He has little eyes and small ears like a mole, too." She blinked a few times. "I guess that's kind of mean. He didn't get to choose the way he looks."

They watched as Monsieur Durand laughed at something Manny had said. Then he pointed toward Chez Jules. Manny shook hands with him and headed in that direction.

Rae and the twins crossed to the other side of the street. They watched as Manny the Mole walked into the restaurant. "You'd think after what Monsieur Durand has been through, he wouldn't want to talk to any criminals ever again," said Rae. "I wonder if he and Manny are getting back into the crime business."

The twins and Rae met up with Mr. Carson and Maxim outside the Centre Pompidou and told them what had happened that afternoon. Maxim was most interested in Manny the Mole. "I bet that rascal is up to no good," he said. "I wonder what he's doing in Paris."

"I don't think we should be so quick to imagine that Martin Durand and Manny the Mole are involved in a crime scheme," replied Mr. Carson. "It sounds as though Martin has made a fine life for himself after he served his time in prison. He may know Manny from years ago. There's no crime in talking to someone."

"He sent Manny to Chez Jules," said Otis. "Why did he do that?"

Mr. Carson rolled his eyes. "Sometimes people go to a restaurant to eat, you know."

"Oh, yeah, right," Otis said. Cody and Rae laughed. "I guess Manny would rather be where they're serving food, instead of *serving time*."

"Very funny," said Mr. Carson, smirking at his son. "I'll tell you what. I'll call Jules and find out if he spoke with Manny." He took his cell phone from his pocket and walked away. He was gone for only a minute, and when he came back he was smiling.

"It turns out that Manny went into Chez Jules and had a salad and a cup of coffee. Then he asked to speak to Jules and was sent to the kitchen. He said he was selling restaurant equipment and asked if Jules needed anything, which he didn't. Nothing to worry about. Let's be glad that Manny straightened himself out. Now let's enjoy the museum."

"So Monsieur Durand just sent Manny to talk to Jules about equipment?" Rae asked her cousins as they walked around the museum. "I guess we got carried away."

"I'm not so sure about that," said Cody.

"Me neither," said Otis. "I'm keeping an eye on that guy. Hey, look at these splatter paintings! I really like them. I'd like to try making one myself."

"I'm sure they're a lot harder to make than they look, but they all appear pretty much the same to me," Maxim said, after they had seen three or four more.

"I understand what you mean, but they're really quite different—and you're right about them being difficult to create," Mr. Carson told him. They started walking again. Up ahead, a man with a hat pulled down over his eyes ran down the stairway. He was carrying a large case in one hand. Shocked onlookers gasped as he shoved them out of the way.

The man pulled on a mask and then threw something. Suddenly the air was full of smoke so thick it was impossible to see anything. People began coughing and running away, rubbing their eyes.

Maxim covered his mouth and nose with a handkerchief. "Keep calm! The exit is over this way."

They hurried out as guards began guiding people toward the doors. Their eyes burned and their throats felt raw. Outside the museum, ambulances were already arriving.

"I'll be okay," Cody said in a scratchy voice. "How about the rest of you?"

The others in the group nodded.

"Smoke bombs generally aren't any more toxic than campfire smoke," Rae said. "Of course, it's not a good idea to stand around breathing them all day."

"Some people might be allergic," Otis added. "It doesn't look like anyone is getting into an ambulance, though."

"That smoke bomb was probably used as a diversion," said Maxim. "In the confusion, I bet that man tried to steal something."

"That's just what I was thinking," Otis said, jamming his hands into his pockets. "I wonder if he got away with it."

"Maybe Uncle Newton will catch him this time," Cody said.

"I hope so," said Mr. Carson.

Maxim cleared his throat. "Well, it looks as if our visit to the Centre Pompidou is finished for the day. I think we should go somewhere and relax, and have some dinner. How about Chez Jules?"

They all agreed enthusiastically. On their way to the café they ran into Jules himself, who was coming out of the shoe repair shop.

"*Bonjour!*" Jules said with a smile. He shifted the

package he was carrying so that he could shake hands with Maxim and Mr. Carson. "I hope you are on your way to my café!"

"Yes, we are," said Mr. Carson. "Detective Andrews will be joining us."

"Ah, yes, I see the detective coming down the street right now. Oh, dear, he does not look too happy. Well, I will see you all inside—sit wherever you like."

The detective was not happy at all. He didn't even touch his meal before he began telling the group about the events of the day. "There were at least two thefts this afternoon," he said. "There might have been more, but the director just won't get it through his head that this is one of the worst crime waves Paris has ever seen. He keeps telling me 'they're only pictures.' These paintings don't mean anything but money to the crooks, but they mean a lot more to people like us who truly appreciate them."

Jules walked over to the table. "*Bonjour*, my friends. I hope you are all enjoying your meals?"

Everyone nodded enthusiastically.

"I like my soup," said Otis, "but when it comes to desserts, you really *take the cake*, Jules."

"Ha ha! Actually, I hired a pastry chef for that. I tried making bread and cakes, but I couldn't *rise* to the occasion."

Otis thought for a moment, then chuckled. "I get it. You put bread dough in a pan and let it rise before you bake it. Nice pun!"

"I know you like puns, so I came up with one for you," said Jules. "It was the *yeast* I could do." He peered at Detective Andrews. "Why do you look so glum, Detective? I've been reading about your investigation in the newspapers. Is it not going well?"

Detective Andrews tore a piece of bread off a baguette halfheartedly. "No." He looked around the table. "Thieves who steal paintings are usually into other kinds of crimes—blackmail, kidnapping, you name it. I wish I could spend more time on these cases. I bet I could have caught the thief already. As it is, he is laughing at me. I found this note on the windshield of my car." He translated the note into English for them as he read it out loud:

It looks like you can't see through my smoke screen, Detective Andrews.

He stuffed the note back in his pocket. "More jokes." He glared at Otis. "What are you laughing about?"

"Sorry," Otis said, feeling guilty. "I was just thinking it was kind of a good pun, that's all. You know, the smoke bomb and the smoke screen. . . ." He stopped talking when he saw that everyone was frowning at him. "Never mind."

Jules stifled a giggle. The detective glared at him. "I'm sorry, Detective Andrews, but Otis has a point. It was kind of funny."

The detective banged his fist on the table. "No, it isn't! I heard about the smoke bomb at the Centre Pompidou, and the director didn't even want me to be part of the investigation! He let some new guy go to work with the guards at the museum!"

"I'm so sorry about these difficulties, Detective Andrews," said Jules. "I will tell the waiter to bring over the dessert cart right away. Maybe that will help to cheer you up."

"I'm just glad that everyone got out of the museum safely," said the detective, attempting to be cheerful in front of his guests. "Now, what's for dessert?"

[Chapter Nine]

Hours later, when everyone else was asleep, Rae and the twins were getting ready for the trip to the catacombs. Rae had brought her backpack into the twins' room. "Everybody got your flashlights and your phones?" She held up her own.

"Yeah," the twins answered. They all shouldered their packs and crept downstairs in the darkness, using their flashlights to find their way. Cody opened the front door carefully and closed it when the others were out. "That was pretty easy. Marcel's car should be at the corner," he said.

Sure enough, when they got to the corner Marcel stuck his hand out of the car window and waved. "Come on, you guys," he called. "You're in for the adventure of your lives."

They all piled into the car, and off they went. "I brought some gear for you," Marcel said. "You'll each find a pair of high rubber boots called hip waders, some miner's hats with headlamps attached, and some slickers. You'll be walking through water once we get underground."

"I didn't even think of that," said Cody. Neither had Otis or Rae. As they sped through Paris, they understood why it was called "The City of Light." Buildings were lit up everywhere: flashbulbs sparkled all over the Eiffel Tower, and strands of lights illuminated the big boats floating along the Seine. "I hope you're not afraid of small, closed-in spaces," Marcel said, glancing at them in the rearview mirror.

"You mean claustrophobic," said Otis. "Not unless we have any *close* calls." He chuckled at his own pun. "No, we've been in plenty of situations that would drive anyone with claustrophobia crazy."

"Good," Marcel chuckled, "because you're going to be in those situations constantly. Most important, and you must all remember this, do not wander away from me, even for a second. You could get lost in the catacombs and never be found. I'm not trying to scare you, but it's true."

"I don't think any of us plan to go off by ourselves, right, guys?" Rae asked.

"Nope," Cody and Otis answered together.

Marcel drove on to where the streets were dark and deserted. "Usually cataphiles, the name for people who love to explore the catacombs, enter through man-holes and climb down long, long ladders. However, my friend Reno found an old entrance in the basement of an abandoned school. He spent some time working for the Catacombs Museum, so he knows all kinds of things about the underbelly of Paris."

Marcel parked the car, and they all got out. The twins and Rae pulled on their hip waders and slickers, and tried on their miner's hats.

"Years ago, people weren't as careful about sealing off the entrances to the catacombs. Now most of the tunnels are off-limits, and every time a new entrance is found the police seal it up. When the school was built, this entrance to the catacombs was just part of the basement."

They switched on their headlamps as they walked toward the old brick schoolhouse. There was the skeleton of an old tree in the weed-choked yard. Marcel led them down some stone steps and pushed open a door.

"We're in the basement," he said. "Head through that archway over there, and get ready to walk down flights of old stone steps for a long time. We're going several stories underground."

"We can run down the steps!" Cody said eagerly.

"No, we can't!" Marcel said firmly. "The steps are slippery, and there is no rail to hold on to. Be careful!"

He was right. The old stone steps *were* slippery. They couldn't go fast, and after what felt like hours, Rae and the twins began to think they would never reach the tunnels. They would just keep finding another flight of steps, then another, and another. Finally, Marcel announced their arrival. "You are now about as far under Paris as anyone can go."

They walked along, hearts beating with anticipation. The air was cool and damp and smelled like earth. The tunnel walls were close on either side of them. Rae stretched out her arms and could brush her fingertips along both walls at the same time. "Moss!" she said, rubbing her fingers on her sleeves. She noticed a plaque dated 1777.

"That must be when this tunnel was built," said Cody. "Look, there's another number: 291."

"The tunnels were assigned numbers for mapping," Marcel told them. "But over the years, the plaques have fallen and the numbers have worn away. It's easy to get lost down here. The first time I came was with Reno—and luckily he knew his way around."

Further along they stood before a stone portal.

Marcel read the inscription above it: "*Arrêtez! C'est içi l'empire de la Mort!* That means, 'Halt! This is the empire of Death!'"

Cody felt a chill run down his spine. Otis shivered, but Rae said, "Cool!"

They passed through the portal. "Oh, wow! Look at this!" Cody said, rubbing his arms to warm them. The entire wall was lined from top to bottom with human skulls. He and his brother stared at it, then looked at each other. "The dream," they both whispered.

The tunnel opened onto a large underground space with a huge pit of water. "There is the friend I came here with the first time," Marcel said. "Hi, Reno!"

Rae and the twins were speechless. Standing in front of them was a tall man in full scuba gear.

"Welcome to the catacombs!" said Reno jovially. "There are lots of pits of water down here. I'm always curious about them," the man explained. He stepped toward the edge of the pit. "This one is pretty deep. I don't know exactly how far down it goes, but I've been to about six meters—that's nearly twenty feet. There are fish living in it!" said Reno. Then he jumped in with a splash.

"Come on, he'll catch up with us later," Marcel told Rae and the twins. "We have a long way to go, and we don't want to miss the party." He led the way through two more low-ceilinged tunnels. The floor became slick with mud, and water sloshed around their boots. About fifteen minutes later, they were out of the muddy water and into another tunnel that curved to the right, then split into two branches. Marcel led Rae and the twins into the one on the left. It was so narrow that they couldn't stretch out their arms. The ceiling got lower and lower until Marcel had to bend his head down. "It doesn't stay like this for long," he assured them.

"That's good," Cody mumbled. He and his brother kept having flashes of their dream. Both were thinking that they wouldn't be able to run very fast through this low, narrow tunnel. Cody imagined the skeleton rattling up behind him and tapping him on the shoulder.

Everyone was glad when the tunnel began to get wider. The ceiling got higher, too, and soon it was so wide that all of them could walk side by side.

"At first, workers were just throwing bones in here to clear out the tunnels they were working on," Marcel said. "Then, later, they decided to neaten things up. Check this out up ahead."

When they saw what he was talking about, Rae and the twins gasped.

"*Whoa!*" Cody said, awestruck. They were looking at rows upon rows of bones on both sides of the tunnel, piled tight as bricks.

"A wall of bones," Otis whispered.

Every other row was packed with skulls. Whoever had come down before them that night had placed candles on rocks along the walls. Embedded in the wall was a large heart shape someone had made from skulls and bones.

"This has got to be one of the spookiest things I've ever seen," Rae said. "Those skulls seem like they're looking right at me."

"I know what you mean," said Marcel. "But they can't hurt you. You'll be seeing a lot more of them, too—Remy says there are around six million skeletons in the catacombs."

"They must be hundreds and hundreds of years old." Cody shivered.

"Definitely," Rae said. "Hey, what a great place for a Halloween party!"

"We've had them down here," Marcel said. "Do you hear that music? We're almost there!"

A couple of minutes later, the tunnel opened into

a huge room with an arched ceiling that soared above them. There were about fifteen people inside, dancing, playing music, and painting. The music was much too loud to allow for introductions, but the guy banging the drums nodded to them. Everyone else smiled, and soon somebody motioned them to join in the dancing. They all took off their hip waders and miner's hats and joined the party.

Cody and Rae danced, but Otis wandered over to where someone was painting an underwater scene on the wall. The mural was gigantic, filled with plants and fish, a dolphin, and even a whale. Otis smiled and gave the artist two thumbs-up. The guy smiled back, reached down and handed him a brush, and nodded. Soon Otis was painting a fish of his own.

When the band took a break, everybody sat around a big table, talking. Rae and the twins liked hearing about how everybody had found out about the catacombs and started coming down underground. "Now *you* are official cataphiles," Marcel told them.

People started leaving, a few at a time. "We might as well get going, too," Marcel said. "I've got to get you guys home before breakfast."

Rae and the twins weren't looking forward to sloshing through the water and climbing the endless flights of steps. They yawned as they pulled on their hip waders and donned their miner's hats.

Cody's legs felt as if they were turning to mud as he splashed through the tunnel full of water. The others kept yelling for him to keep up, but he could hardly keep his eyes open. At some point when they were heading for the flights of steps, he leaned against a wall and nearly dozed off standing up.

He hurried to catch up to the group. He thought he saw them up ahead, but it turned out to be just some rocks and shadows. He found that he had stumbled into the wrong tunnel. He backtracked and turned into a different one, calling out, "Rae, Otis, Marcel!"

No answer. All he heard was dripping water and the sound of something scurrying across the dirt floor. He kept looking at the bones lining the walls and remembering his dream. He almost thought he could hear the skeleton rattling behind him. Cody told himself to keep calm. The others couldn't be far away. They would miss him soon and come back for him.

At first Cody tried to stand still and wait, but each second that went by seemed to take an hour. He started walking again, hurrying along. He came to the open area they had passed before, where the skulls and bones were piled high.

The skulls seemed to grin at him. As he looked at them, he began to think of how many skeletons from hundreds of years were stored in the catacombs. He didn't believe in ghosts, but it was hard not to in a place full of skulls.

What was that noise? It sounded like someone sighing—and crying. Cody began to shiver. "Who's there?" he called. "Marcel? Is something wrong?"

"I've been waiting for you," came the answer in an eerie, hollow voice. "At last you're here."

"W-what do you mean you've been waiting for me? Quit fooling around, guys. I'm tired, and I want to go home."

"You're not leaving; you're going to stay here with me. I have a present for you."

Then a figure stepped out of the shadows, its long cloak sweeping the ground. The cloak covered the figure's head completely so Cody couldn't see a face. Cody's blood turned to ice when he saw that the hand clutching the cloak was made of bones. The figure was a skeleton!

Cody's heart thumped so hard he was afraid it would burst through his chest. The dream had been *real*! "This is for you." The skeleton stretched out a bony hand holding a skull. "Take it. It's *yours*."

[Chapter Ten]

"**A**hh!" Cody cried out as he woke up. He was trembling. *Where is the skeleton?* he wondered. He clutched the covers fearfully as his eyes darted around the room. He could feel himself blushing as he realized he'd just been having another nightmare. He looked over at his brother's bed and was glad to see that Otis had already gone down to breakfast.

Cody saw his hip waders in a corner. He was still wearing his clothes from last night. *So I have been down to the catacombs after all,* he realized. *I mixed up reality and fantasy in my nightmare—how weird!*

He felt grimy and hurried to the shower. As he dried and put on clean clothes, he wondered if the grown-ups had any idea that he and the others had sneaked out last night.

He went downstairs and found everyone else, including Uncle Newton, finishing breakfast.

"Hi, everybody. Sorry I'm so late. I guess I was pretty tired last night."

"Yes, I imagine so." Maxim peeked from behind his newspaper. "How was your trip to the catacombs? Otis and Rae were just telling us how exciting it was."

Cody looked at Otis and Rae. They both shrugged.

"You really thought I had no idea what was going on?" Mr. Carson shook his head. "I'm surprised at the three of you. You're usually such good detectives. How do you think Marcel came up with hip waders and other gear in just your size?"

Cody felt his face turning red. "Oh. Was that what those errands were about?"

"Mmm–hmm." Maxim smiled.

"You almost didn't get to go," said Mr. Carson. He took a sip from his cup of coffee. "You should thank Marcel for doing such a good job of convincing me that you'd all be safe. Then I had to make a call to get an okay from Rae's mother. I think she was harder to convince than I was."

Cody shifted in his chair. "Thanks, Dad. Why didn't you tell us you knew?"

Mr. Carson gazed at the ceiling for a moment. "Oh, I just thought it would be even more exciting if you thought you were sneaking out this time. I remember one time when I was a boy . . . Oh, never mind. Anyway, that was a one-time-only event. Don't ever pull a stunt like that again!"

Cody and Otis had never seen their dad look so fierce.

Maxim coughed so suddenly he spit out some of his coffee. Everyone jumped. Maxim was always so perfectly composed.

"Don't worry, I'm fine." Maxim dabbed at the coffee with a napkin. He quickly turned the page of his newspaper.

"I bet I know what you just saw," the detective said glumly. "Was it something on page eight?"

Maxim nodded slowly. "I'm so sorry."

"I might as well tell everybody, because they'll find out sooner or later," said Detective Andrews. "The thief put a note in the paper, congratulating himself on stealing another painting yesterday. He talks a lot about how I'm a bumbling fool and I'll never catch him," he said. "He called me 'Andrews the Donkey' and said I couldn't find my own behind."

"Oooh, that's bad," said Cody.

The detective nodded. "What's almost worse is that the newspaper must have been given the note even before the thief stole the painting. The editor said they get that section ready to print the day before. The thief was so sure he would succeed that he delivered the note in advance."

Detective Andrews raked a hand through his gray hair. "One of the guards who was interviewed at the Centre Pompidou said they'd had some trouble a week ago. Someone broke all the mirrors in three different bathrooms. The guard thought that it was some kind of bad omen." Detective Andrews shrugged.

That's shattering *news*, thought Otis. He knew better than to repeat the pun aloud.

This is terrible," said Mr. Carson. "Surely the Paris police will take these thefts more seriously now. After all, the thief isn't just taunting you. He's making fun of the entire police department."

The detective poured himself another cup of coffee. "You'd think so, wouldn't you? I talked to the director about it this morning, as soon as I saw the note in the paper. He wants me to go looking for a diplomat's lost dog. And I have no choice in the matter—my boss at Scotland Yard says I'm under the Paris police director's jurisdiction." He slapped his forehead. "There is a crime wave in the city and I have to hunt down a lost dog! As if it were an international incident. . . ."

"Well, I hope you find the dog," Rae said.

"Thank you," the detective said sourly. "I'm sorry about the lost pooch, but I should be working on crimes! That note in the paper isn't the end of the thief's little jokes. He sent me an e-mail, too, informing me that there is a big theft to come. Unfortunately, the e-mail message was sent from the public library, so I couldn't trace the exact sender."

Just then, the detective's phone started ringing.

"Excuse me, I have to take this call," he said. He got up from the table and left the kitchen. Moments later he was back, shaking with rage.

"Can you believe this? A splatter painting was stolen from the Centre Pompidou yesterday and replaced with a forgery. Guards only just noticed it. I would have known right away. And get this: the director tells me I still have to find the missing dog before I can investigate the theft case any further!"

After breakfast, the Carson bunch headed to the Musée d'Orsay, where they lunched in a beautiful museum cafe. There were paintings on the walls, and floor-to-ceiling windows were hung with red velvet drapes. Crystal chandeliers sparkled overhead.

"Did you know this museum was once a railroad station?" Rae asked the twins.

"That's kind of cool," said Otis.

Cody didn't reply. He was too busy looking at the array of desserts, arranged on a table with two huge silver bowls of whipped cream. All through the meal he had been stealing glances at the table in anticipation.

"We won't be here all day, Cody," said Maxim.

"Okay, okay," Cody said, and chose a piece of cake topped with a generous dollop of whipped cream. When he'd finished it, he leaned back and sighed. "I think the desserts here are as good as the ones at Chez Jules," he said. "I'd better try some more at different places around the city just to be sure."

"Don't forget that we're here to do more than eat pastry," said Mr. Carson as he paid the bill. When they left the restaurant and walked into the museum, they were surprised to find Detective Andrews talking with employees. He saw the Carson group and nodded.

"Thank goodness I found the dog before we got the call from the museum," he said. "They discovered that a painting was stolen from a storage room today. They don't know how long it has been missing." He turned to a white-haired woman who worked there. "Do you remember seeing anyone suspicious?"

She shook her head. "I can't think of a thing."

"So how did you discover that a painting was missing from the storage area?" he asked.

"I was checking inventory. Some of the paintings had been put in storage temporarily, because we were planning to move them to a new location in the museum. There was *Woman with a Black Boa* by Toulouse-Lautrec, and—"

"Why was the painting in storage?" Otis interrupted. "Did it fall off the wall because it was *too loose*? Get it? *Toulouse . . . too loose?*"

Cody and Rae groaned. Detective Andrews chuckled. "Good one, Otis, but no more puns for now." He turned back to the woman. "Was that the painting that was stolen?"

"No," said the woman, giving Otis a stern look. "It was a Van Gogh self-portrait. I've been working here for forty years, and I know a real Van Gogh when I see one! It's very odd, though. The thief left a peculiar new portrait in its place."

"Please show it to me," said Detective Andrews.

"I'll get it," she told him. She disappeared into the storage area and returned holding a large framed picture. Before she handed it to him, she gave the detective the strangest look.

As soon as Detective Andrews saw it, his face turned purple with rage.

"This thief has gone too far now! I'm taking this with me as evidence," he sputtered. "Let's go," he said to Rae and the twins. He nodded to the woman. "That's all for now. Thank you."

"Be careful not to brush against the walls as you leave," she said. "We've just had several holes repaired. The plaster hasn't been painted over so it's very powdery and could come off on your clothes. It's happened to me twice already." She gestured to two white smudges on the sleeve of her dark-green blouse.

"Can we see the painting, Uncle Newton?" Cody asked as they walked out of the museum.

"Oh, all right," he said after a moment. He turned the picture around so that Rae and the twins could see it. It was obvious that the portrait was of the detective himself. He was wearing a Roman toga and holding a chicken under one arm. The thief had played another joke on Detective Andrews!

[Chapter Eleven]

The detective managed to keep his cool until he left the museum. Maxim and the others followed him out to his car. Detective Andrews put the portrait in the trunk. Then he found a note on his windshield:

I hope you enjoy your new piece of art: a portrait of the world's dumbest detective.

"Arrgh!" The detective threw the note on the ground and stomped on it with his feet. "That blasted rat! The nerve of that guy! Wait until I get my hands on him!" He began jumping up and down.

"Uncle Newton, I think you'd better stop that," said Cody. "People are looking at you. The thief may be one of them. You never know."

The detective stood still and looked around. People in the parking lot were gawking at him. He straightened up and patted his hair. Then he picked up the note and put it in his pocket.

"I'll see you later," he said in a dignified manner. He got into his car and slammed the door.

The detective rolled down the window. "The most frustrating thing about this case isn't the fact that the director doesn't think it's important, or even the jokes. It's the methods. Most thieves get lazy and use the same method over and over. Not this guy. He puts tape over a lock, throws smoke bombs, tries breaking and entering. What's next? I have no idea!" He rolled up the window and drove away.

Later that night, Cody and Otis went to bed but stayed up for hours. They talked about the art theft. "Maybe it isn't one thief but a ring of thieves," Otis offered.

"If it is, there has to be a ringleader, right? I guess it could be a few copycats acting on their own, but I don't really think so," Cody said thoughtfully. "What we'd have to figure out to be sure is the link between the crimes."

"What if there isn't a link?" Otis asked. He opened his mouth to say something else but stopped, listening. "Did you hear that, Cody?"

"Uh-huh. It sounds like someone just stumbled into a garbage can outside."

They got up and went to the window. In the

moonlight, they could see a shadow moving across the little garden behind their uncle's apartment building.

"What do you want to do?" Cody asked.

"Let's make sure no one gets in," said Otis.

The two of them crept downstairs. They listened for sounds of someone trying to break in. They never heard them. After about twenty minutes, they went back up to bed.

"Maybe somebody just got lost," Cody said.

"I guess it's possible," said Otis. "I don't really think so though, do you?"

"Not really. But I'm too tired to think anymore. I've got to get some sleep. Good night, Otis."

The next morning when Rae and the twins came downstairs, Maxim and Mr. Carson were sitting at the breakfast table. The detective had already gone to work. As usual, Maxim was reading the morning paper. "Tonight," he noted, "is the last night that the collection of skull paintings will be exhibited at the Louvre Museum. They are on loan from galleries and museums from all over the world."

Otis furrowed his brows. "Skull paintings at the Louvre? I thought they only had really *old* paintings."

"These skull paintings *are* very old—most of them

were painted in the 1600s," Maxim said, peering over the newspaper. "The collection is called Memento Mori. It's a Latin phrase that means 'remember your mortality.'"

"It would be cool to see paintings of skulls," said Cody.

"Yeah," Otis agreed. "Let's go today."

Mr. Carson looked at his watch. "I'm afraid I won't be able to join you. I'm supposed to be giving art lectures for most of the day. Then there is the opening of a new gallery and a big party afterward. In between, I'll only have time to change clothes. The rest of you can go to the museum."

"Oh, I wish I could," said Maxim regretfully. "But I promised an old friend who lives outside of town that I'd spend the day with him. It's been so long since we've seen each other, and I don't want to cancel. I'll be back for the party later, of course."

Cody and Otis were helping themselves to the rolls that their uncle had left for everyone. "We forgot that today was the day you were lecturing, Dad," said Cody. "We'll be okay by ourselves."

"I know," said Mr. Carson. "Your uncle is going to the party as well. His housekeeper, Ida, will be coming to make dinner for you and stay until we get home. I'm going to call a couple of times during the day on my breaks. Make sure you have your phones on."

"Okay, Dad," said Cody. He turned to the others. "Let's get ready to go."

As soon as they were out of the room, Cody snapped his fingers. "I've got a hunch. All of the paintings that have been stolen were famous, or at least well known, and expensive. The thief takes big risks. Maybe stealing from little galleries without security systems isn't such a big risk. Stealing from the Centre Pompidou and the Musée d'Orsay *is*."

Otis's face lit up. "Right! It's like he enjoys showing how far he can go and taunting Uncle Newton about it. Are you thinking what I'm thinking?" He and his brother looked at each other and nodded.

"I get it," Rae said. "There's a good chance that he'll try to steal one of the skull paintings from the Louvre Museum tonight, before the show closes." She thought for a moment. "I don't think he would try to do it in the daytime. The Louvre has one of the best security systems in the world—heat sensors, motion detectors, cameras all over the place, and plenty of guards around the clock. There aren't as many guards at night, though."

She thought for a moment. "The security system is really cool. Each of the paintings has a motion sensor on it that can detect the tiniest movement. Another sensor is attached to the back of the frame. That one sends out a signal every fifteen seconds, tracking the exact location of the painting."

"That *is* pretty cool," said Otis. "I wonder how a thief could get around all that."

"Wait—I'm not finished. There are sensors on the windows and doors, too. The alarm system is huge. The thief would never try to steal the *Mona Lisa*. They keep that one behind bulletproof glass. The *Mona Lisa* has special guards, too."

"Wow. The museum is open until almost ten o'clock tonight. The thief will probably try to grab the painting after that. How are we going to manage to be there without getting caught?" Otis asked.

Cody crossed his arms. "I don't know if this is such a great idea. Can you imagine what Dad, and Maxim, and Uncle Newton would do if we got caught? They'd really love the idea that we broke into the Louvre," he said sarcastically.

Rae and Otis thought for a moment. A smile broke out on Rae's face. "We won't break in," she said. "We'll be there before it closes. Then we'll hide and wait for the thief afterward."

"I think we owe it to Uncle Newton," Otis said. "This case is driving him crazy. I hate the way the thief humiliates him. He can't do that to our uncle and get away with it!"

"I agree," said Rae firmly. "We've got to get that thief."

Cody sighed. "Still sounds crazy and dangerous, but if you guys are determined to do this, we should go this afternoon and find out where the paintings are. We'll scope out places to hide. Then we'll come back here, pretend that everything is normal, and when the housekeeper thinks we're asleep, we'll go back to the museum before it closes." He was warming to the idea. "We can put pillows under the bedcovers to make it look like there are bodies in the beds. We'll have to hope that if the housekeeper checks on us, she'll just open the door and look in. And we'll be sure to be home before Dad, Maxim, and Uncle Newton get back from the party."

"Good plan," said Otis.

"Now we have one big problem left. We know how we're getting in," said Cody. "How do we get *out*?"

[Chapter Twelve]

When Otis, Cody, and Rae went to the Louvre Museum that afternoon, they noticed an area where workers were coming and going. The men entered the area in uniforms and came out in street clothes.

"There's probably a bathroom in there. It's possible that there wouldn't be an alarm on that window since it isn't for the public," said Cody.

"Dream on," Rae said. "I think when a museum installs an alarm system, they include *every* door and window."

Cody shook his head. "Uncle Newton told us that there were some weaknesses in the security and that people were getting careless lately. I'm going in to have a look. I don't see any more men coming out."

"Hurry, and be careful!" Rae said. "I don't see anybody looking this way. Go!"

Cody entered the work area, and Otis and Rae waited nervously. They pretended to be looking at nearby paintings, trying not to attract attention as their hearts pounded. Luckily, everyone in the gallery seemed focused on the art.

When Cody returned, Otis and Rae could see that beads of sweat stood out on his forehead.

"*Whew!* That was scary, but it paid off. There's a locker room for the workmen in there, and a bathroom . . . with an open window we can crawl through!"

Otis wiped his sweaty palms on his pants. "Let's hope it's still open when we need it."

"I think it's our best shot. We'll have to check the window when we come back tonight. Let's go see the skull paintings," said Rae. She studied a map of the museum. "This is lucky. They're not far from here. Follow me."

Rae led them to the nearby gallery. Each painting there was a highly realistic still life. The artists had painted skulls resting alone in cabinets, sitting on books or papers like grotesque paperweights, or positioned with objects such as hourglasses, watches, wilted flowers, or decaying fruit. A member of the museum staff was giving a lecture about the paintings in French, but another was giving one in English. A group of people had gathered around her.

"This last painting on our tour is called *Still Life with a Skull*," the guide explained. "It was painted in the first half of the seventeenth century by Philippe de Champaigne, an artist born and trained in Brussels. Notice how the light is reflected off the glass vase, and how it illuminates the withering tulip. If you look closely, you will see that everything shown here symbolizes the passage of time and death, to remind the viewer that life is short and that time must be used wisely. Philippe de Champaigne's work is in museums throughout the world and is *very* popular with private collectors. This painting is on loan and this is its last night at the Louvre—you are fortunate to have the opportunity to see it! I hope you have enjoyed the tour. Please feel free to remain in the gallery as long as you like."

"Sheesh. These paintings are depressing—and creepy!" said Otis as the tour group broke up and began leaving the gallery. "Too bad we missed the beginning of her talk. Let's take a closer look at the picture."

"I really like it," said Cody, leaning in and admiring the details. "You can see what the guide meant about the light—like it's streaming through a window and right into the painting."

"Don't get any closer than this," said Rae, pointing to a railing that ran low around the walls. "It's a motion sensor, and it wouldn't take much to trip the alarm."

"I wonder how the thief will deal with *that*," muttered Otis. Then he turned to Cody and said under his breath, "These paintings *remind* you of anything?"

"Uh-huh," Cody answered. "I had that nightmare again."

"Me, too," said Otis. "Isn't it weird that we dreamed about the catacombs before we'd even seen them?"

"Definitely freaky," answered his brother.

"Earth to cousins!" said Rae, looking exasperated. "We don't have much time! Did you hear the guide say that this artist is really popular with private collectors now? This could be the painting the thief will try to steal."

"Could be," said Otis. "Let's study the map later so we'll be able to find that bathroom with our eyes closed. The thief, or guards, might be chasing us, and we all need to know exactly where we're going. Right now we need to find a hiding place for tonight."

They found it in an area not far away, where furniture was displayed from different periods of history. "We can hide in these big antique trunks," Rae said. She looked to see if any guards or visitors were watching, then she stepped close to one. She held her breath and opened the lid.

"*Whew!* No alarm went off. We can get in here

when it gets close to ten. We'll wait a while, and then peek out to check for guards before we try to get near the painting. We'll have to be really, really careful because there will be guards all over the place."

"You're right about that, Rae," Cody agreed. "I hope they don't have lasers crisscrossing the halls at night."

"They probably have them in some places. I don't think they have them everywhere though," she said. "How could the guards walk around without alarms going off every minute?"

"She could be right," said Otis. "It could be one of those weak points in security that Uncle Newton mentioned." Otis watched some men carrying equipment up ahead. "Let's go see what they're doing."

They followed the men down the steps and through a hallway. At the end of the hall, they turned left into another section of the museum that contained several rooms on either side and one huge room at the end. The men were so busy that they didn't notice Cody, Otis, and Rae at first. Then a couple of workers carried some furniture and computers into the room.

"Why are you moving all this stuff?" Cody asked one of the workers.

The man rolled his eyes. "The place just got repainted, so we had to take everything out. Now we're putting everything back. Speaking of putting things back, put yourselves back upstairs. You kids shouldn't be down here."

"We were just curious. Sorry to bother you! Let's go, guys," Cody said.

"Did you see all the computers in that room?" whispered Rae as they climbed the stairs. "I'll bet there were a hundred."

"There were a lot, for sure," said Otis. "That must have been the main hub of the security center. They take security pretty seriously here. I don't think this would be an easy place to get into."

"No, but this thief is so full of himself he might try," said Rae. "Now let's go work on our plan."

Cody smiled as he muttered one of his favorite palindromes, "*A man, a plan, a canal, Panama.*"

Detective Andrews's housekeeper, Ida Bernard, arrived at his house at six o'clock. She was grandmotherly and very nice. She made a delicious dinner for Rae and the twins.

"Your father said you all like the French pastry, especially you, Cody," she said after they had eaten. She produced a box tied with string. "He suggested I bring you some from Chez Jules."

"*Très bien!* Very good! *Merci!*" Cody said happily.

Madame Bernard was so nice that they all felt a little guilty about having to trick her.

After dessert, Rae, Cody, and Otis began yawning and saying how sleepy they were. Madame Bernard wished them all a good night's rest, and they trooped up the stairs to their rooms. After going over the plan one more time, Rae and the twins disguised their beds with plumped pillows under the covers. Then, as quietly as they could, they crept out the door.

"My heart is pounding as hard as when we snuck out to go to the catacombs!" Rae whispered.

"You don't have to whisper, Rae. The housekeeper can't hear us now," Cody told her.

Rae laughed nervously.

Otis checked his watch. "It's eight-thirty now. Let's synchronize our watches and phones. We should be there by quarter to nine. I'm afraid that if we go too late we might not get in—or it would look suspicious. When the crowd begins thinning out later, we'll check that bathroom window. Then we can get into our trunks and hide."

They hurried on their way. The streets around the Louvre were crowded with people. "Remember, we keep calm and stick with the plan," said Rae. The twins nodded.

The tired worker at the museum's entrance barely looked at them as they flashed the museum passes they'd bought earlier. Once they were inside the museum, they started to sweat. This was the first time they'd hidden out in a public place, let alone in the most famous art gallery in the world. "We're in the big leagues now!" Otis said.

They found a bunch of people crowded around the skull paintings. Rae and the twins checked out everyone around them. None of the tourists looked suspicious.

Uniformed guards began asking people to clear the galleries about fifteen minutes before closing time. Everyone began moving slowly toward exits marked *Sortie*. Rae and the twins slipped into the workers' locker area. They had decided to hide in the bathroom stalls there until the museum was closed. When they were sure all the visitors had left they could sneak into the trunks.

"We're in luck," Cody whispered, pointing up. "The window is still open!"

They each picked a stall and hid, sitting on the toilet seats with their feet pulled up in case anyone checked underneath the doors.

They waited for complete silence, and then peeked outside cautiously. A guard passed by, whistling a tune.

When they were sure he was gone, they made their way to their trunks. Once inside, they had to wait some more. They had agreed on twenty minutes.

Cody found that his neck hurt after about five minutes. He could move only a little bit. Soon he got a cramp in his left leg, then his right. He kept checking the time on his phone. The minutes dragged by. The others were having the same trouble.

When twenty minutes had passed, they each lifted their trunk lids and peeked out. The coast was clear. One by one, they climbed out of their cramped quarters. As soon as they stood up they all found that they had become a little dazed from the lack of air in the trunks. They shook their heads and staggered a little as they stretched their arms and legs.

Cody held a finger to his lips, signaling for quiet. The others nodded and followed him down the dim hallway, walking carefully on their unsteady legs. They hadn't thought that it would feel so strange to be in an empty museum.

It wasn't completely empty, though. They rounded a corner and saw a guard walking up ahead with his back to them. They ducked swiftly into the gallery of skull paintings and flattened themselves against the wall. They did their best to silence their ragged breathing. Everywhere they looked, skulls glowed an eerie white on their dark canvases.

Otis peered around the corner and nodded to the others. "No guards now. Let's hide under that sofa as we planned. Remember, if the thief sees us, he won't make a move."

What the three didn't know was that, at that very moment, the thief was exiting a storage room holding a laptop computer. He knelt down and punched some keys on the keyboard. He looked up at a video camera and smiled broadly. He had just sent commands to a computer in the main security area. It controlled the video cameras in certain wings of the museum, and he had just frozen them. Next, he disabled the motion sensor rail and the sensors on the paintings, too. He chuckled as he closed the laptop and slipped it into his backpack. Everything was ready.

Rae and the twins were positioned underneath the sofa when they heard footsteps entering the gallery. It took less than a minute for the thief to get some tools from his backpack and pry a painting from the wall. Rae looked at her cousins wide-eyed. Why hadn't the alarm gone off? The three of them held their breath, but each of them was wondering how they could get a good look at the thief before he escaped. From their hiding place, they couldn't see the thief—they could only hear the quiet scrape of his tools.

In the control room, rows of people were seated at monitors. The screens showed views of all locations in the museum. One of the operators laughed when a guard gave a thumbs-up toward the camera as he passed. "My guy always passes his checkpoint right on time," he said.

"These guards sure have the timing down perfectly," another operator said. In the back of the room an operator was only half looking at his screen. He had skipped dinner and was very hungry. He took a sandwich from a brown bag and began to eat.

When he was halfway through the sandwich, he began to get a sinking feeling. He hadn't seen a guard pass on his video screen. He noticed that the image on the screen looked too still, like a photo instead of a live image. He punched some keys, but the image remained still.

"My monitor is frozen," he said. "It's the camera in the Memento Mori gallery!" he cried. He radioed guards in the area.

Rae and the twins heard the voices of guards on walkie-talkies, and they could see their black work boots as they thundered past the gallery. There were so many of them!

Cody, Otis, and Rae were all trembling. They were just about to crawl out from underneath the sofa when they saw a pair of shoes. Someone was tiptoeing by, and it wasn't a guard. Those shoes weren't work boots. They were soft and shiny, and they looked very special and expensive.

An alarm was beginning to sound in Otis's mind. The only kind of thief who would wear shoes like that when pulling a heist was someone who cared about shoes *a lot*. And he definitely knew someone who fit *that* profile—Martin Durand, the art framer. Otis carefully removed his smartphone from his back pocket, made sure the flash was turned off, and snapped a silent photo of the thief's shoes. *Gotcha*, he thought.

Just then the sound of *real* alarms ripped through the air. The screech of metal gates crashing down soon followed. The wearer of the shiny shoes raced away.

"We'd better move it before we get trapped in here," Cody said in a panic.

They squeezed out from underneath the sofa and began running down the hall. Any second, they expected a bunch of museum guards to grab them. "I think we can make it to the bathroom with the open window!" Rae said, pointing.

They skidded into the workers' bathroom. They could hear the guards outside in the hallway. One by one, Rae and the twins pulled themselves through the window and dropped to the other side. The sight of guards patrolling the museum grounds told them they weren't free yet. They crouched behind some bushes, trying to blend in with the shadows. It seemed like forever before the area outside the museum was clear enough to get away.

"I can't believe how super lucky we were," Cody panted as they raced toward Uncle Newton's house. "What a close call. I think—"

"Shhh! Not now, Cody," Otis hissed. "Keep your mind on running *away*, not running your *mouth*!"

[Chapter Thirteen]

Luck was definitely on their side that night. Rae and the twins got into their pajamas without so much as a squeak in the floorboards to wake a sleeper. They had barely gotten into their beds before they were sound asleep themselves.

The next morning when Rae and the twins went downstairs, Mr. Carson and Maxim were sitting at the kitchen table. Maxim was reading the paper, and Mr. Carson was drinking coffee. The housekeeper, Ida Bernard, was gathering her things to leave.

"Jules brought some breakfast pastries earlier," she said when she saw Rae and the twins. "They're on the counter. I know you like them the most, Cody." She smiled warmly at him and put on her jacket.

Otis and Rae said good-bye to her. When it was Cody's turn, he seized the opportunity to make a new palindrome. "*So, Ida, adios,*" he said, grinning broadly.

Otis and Rae rolled their eyes. The housekeeper looked confused. "*Au revoir,*" she said, then left.

When the detective walked into the kitchen, he looked even more depressed than the day before. "Show them the picture in the paper, Maxim," he said.

"Someone tried to take a painting from the Louvre last night. The thief had to leave it behind while making his getaway. The guards found it stashed behind a statue. This time he didn't have a chance to leave one of his forgeries, either."

Detective Andrews sighed. "I'd like to say that it means he's not as clever as he thinks he is. However, we still haven't caught him, and he's managed to make us look like fools again. A video camera caught this picture."

Maxim put the newspaper on the table.

"That's definitely our joker," said the detective glumly.

Rae and the twins looked at the picture of someone wearing a clown mask. "A video camera caught this as the thief was leaving the museum. One of the security people said there was a glitch and the camera near the painting malfunctioned."

"Which painting did the thief try to steal?" Rae asked innocently.

"Let's see . . . yes, here it is," said Maxim, looking

more closely at the caption of a photograph in the newspaper. "It's called *Still Life with a Skull*. Did you happen to see it on your visit to the Louvre yesterday?"

Rae and the twins glanced at each other. "Uh-huh," Otis said.

"It was really beautiful," Rae added. "I'm glad the thief didn't get away with stealing it."

"They've *got* to tighten up security at the Louvre." The detective shook his head. "I told them there were weak spots. They should be checking and rechecking those cameras all the time. Maybe we would have seen the thief without the mask or gotten something else to go on. I just don't understand it." He put his coffee cup in the sink. "I have to get to the office. Maybe I'll get my big break today and finally catch this guy. Bye for now."

"At least the thief didn't get the painting," Cody said as the detective closed the front door behind himself.

"True," Mr. Carson said. "But your uncle is no closer to catching him. It's driving him nuts."

There was the sound of sirens outside, getting closer and closer, until the blaring was deafening. It stopped right in front of the house. Everyone ran to the window and was shocked to see Detective Andrews being handcuffed. They all ran outside.

"What's going on?" Mr. Carson asked a police officer with a red mustache.

"I have been authorized to arrest Detective Andrews for the theft of several paintings, and for breaking into the Louvre last night." The officer produced a piece of paper. "I also have a warrant to search his property," he snapped.

Detective Andrews's face was pale. "How can this be? This is ridiculous! On what grounds do you suspect me?"

"Anonymous tip," the officer said shortly.

"But this is impossible," sputtered Mr. Carson. "I was with the detective all evening at a party. Hundreds of people saw him!"

The officer with the search warrant in his hand pushed Mr. Carson aside as another police car drove up. "Please do not interfere with our investigation, monsieur. Here comes our computer expert," he said.

The officer took Detective Andrews back inside the house and pushed him roughly into a chair. Then the officer and his partner began searching the house. They opened all the cupboards and closets. "You won't find anything here," Detective Andrews called. "I've worked as a detective for fifteen years. Why would I start stealing art?"

The officer acted as though he hadn't heard him. "I'm going upstairs," he told his partner. "Let me know if the tech finds anything on the detective's laptop. It's on that table near the kitchen."

The Carsons, Maxim, and Rae watched in stunned silence as a man with thinning hair and thick glasses brought the computer into the kitchen and booted up. Soon he was tap-tap-tapping away.

"You won't find anything incriminating in there," the detective told him. "This is absurd. I demand to speak to Director Brun. He'll put a stop to this."

The man looked at Detective Andrews through his thick glasses. "It was Brun who gave the order," he said. Then he tapped on the keyboard some more. "Ah," he said. "Ah."

The other officer came downstairs. "I found nothing so far," he said to his partner. "Let's check the basement." He turned to the man at the computer. "Did you find anything of interest?"

"Oh, yes," he said, nodding. "I'm finding *lots* of interesting things."

Rae and the twins gasped. "There must be some mistake!" said Mr. Carson.

The officer ignored him and left. He came back a few minutes later and spoke quietly in French with the guy at the computer. Then he straightened up and glared at Detective Andrews. "We have what we came for. Your computer is loaded with evidence. You've hidden it cleverly, but our expert found it all."

"There was nothing to find!" Detective Andrews said frantically.

"Oh yes, there was," the officer insisted. "There are floor plans of all of the art museums in Paris with escape routes and detailed notes. There are drawings of the security systems, lists of stolen paintings, as well as those you were plotting to steal, complete with notes about black market prices beside them! We have the contents of the message in the newspaper and other messages you claimed the thief sent to you. You've even drafted other notes to go along with future thefts. Now you won't need to use them."

"Can't you see I'm being framed?" Detective Andrews protested.

Yeah, I get the picture, Otis punned to himself. He couldn't believe what was happening.

The officer snorted. "Still trying to deny your guilt? You're a crook. I just found the stolen paintings right down there in the basement."

Rae and the twins exchanged looks of shock and disbelief. "This is all part of a plot to incriminate Detective Andrews," said Maxim.

"Of course it is!" Detective Andrews thundered. He looked at the officer who had called him a crook. "You're going to regret this."

Mr. Carson hurried to the detective's side. "Don't worry, Newton," he said. "I'm sure this is just some kind of crazy mistake. We'll get this all sorted out."

"I'm sure you're right. I'll get to the bottom of this," said the detective.

"Well, it looks like you'll have to do it from jail, unless you can explain why all that evidence is in your computer and in your basement. It looks like you used your position to get inside information. It helped you steal. You're a disgrace to the police department."

The officer's partner was looking more and more uncomfortable. He fired off angry sentences in French to the policeman with the red mustache. Rae and the twins understood enough to know that he felt his partner had gone too far.

The policeman looked away, but he didn't apologize. "This man stole France's prized paintings," he said firmly. "I don't care who he is or how long he's been a detective."

"But our uncle hasn't been found guilty." Cody crossed his arms over his chest and glared at the officer.

"I want to see these paintings that you claim I stole," said Detective Andrews.

The officer with the red mustache shrugged. "Why not? You can all come and have a look."

They followed the officers into the hallway and downstairs to the basement below the building. There were two entrances to the basement—one from inside the apartment building, and one from the garden. There was a stack of paintings on a long bench. "We found these under a drop cloth," said the officer with the attitude. "Guess what? These are the paintings that were reported stolen, all seven of them. Look, here's the Van Gogh portrait." He held up the painting on top of the stack.

Cody snorted. "If that's your proof, then our uncle is *definitely* not guilty. That's a fake. In the real painting, Van Gogh's beard is as red as your mustache. And the brush strokes in the background aren't quite right."

Rae whipped out her smartphone and did an image search for "Van Gogh self-portraits." "See for yourself," Rae said to the officer, turning the screen to face him.

"You're absolutely right, both of you," said Mr. Carson. He examined the other paintings in the stack. "I believe these are all forgeries. Someone has the real paintings, and it isn't my brother-in-law."

The nasty officer sneered. "The thief puts forgeries

in place of the real art. As far as I'm concerned, this proves our guy is guilty. He—or a partner in crime—must have practiced to get the forgeries just right. These could be the rejects. Now we'll have to get him to tell us what happened to the real ones."

"But the twins heard someone prowling around outside in the garden behind the apartment the other night. Whoever that was could have planted the paintings in the basement. We noticed there is an entrance to the basement back there." Rae protested. "The thief who put those notes in the newspaper is out to get Detective Andrews."

"Nice try, kid," the officer replied. He put a hand on the detective's shoulder. "Come along now. I have to take you to the police station. I never thought I would put a detective in jail."

"Don't worry, I won't be gone long," said the detective to the group before he was escorted to the waiting police car. An officer carrying some paintings followed, and he made two more trips for the remaining paintings and the computer.

Maxim and the rest of the Carson bunch watched as the police car drove away. Rae and the twins stayed outside when Mr. Carson and Maxim went back into the house to make phone calls. That was the first time they noticed that Marcel and Monsieur Durand were standing across the street. The two men waved hello to them.

"What are *they* doing here?" Otis turned quickly to Cody and Rae. "We'd better find that thief fast," he said, "or our uncle is *French toast*. Did you see how that officer wasn't even surprised that the paintings were forgeries? It's like he knew all along."

"I thought that was weird, too," said Rae. "The whole thing looks like your uncle was set up and the cop in the mustache knew all about it."

"That's what I think," said Otis. "Uncle Newton was *framed* and *nailed*." He snapped his fingers. "Remember that e-mail he got from the thief? The e-mail could have had a link embedded. When he clicked on the link, it could have transferred information onto his hard drive. I've heard about hackers doing stuff like that."

"I think I follow you," Cody said. "There could have been a secret program in the page. It downloaded into Uncle Newton's computer, just like a virus. Then it began downloading the suspicious files to his computer without him knowing. It stored the files in a secret place that he didn't know about either."

Rae was nodding. "Yeah, so it looked like he had hidden the files," she said.

"Hidden, yes, but not so hidden that a computer expert couldn't find them," said Otis. His eyes narrowed a bit "Especially if he knew what he was looking for." He turned to his brother. "I don't know if the officer knew all about the files before he *found* them. But I have a bad feeling about the director our uncle is working with. According to that computer expert, it was Director Brun who ordered the arrest."

"Right," Cody said. "I don't think the new director is as clueless as he seems about art theft. How could the director of the police department think a diplomat's missing dog or a stolen cameo brooch is more important than the theft of important paintings worth lots of money? It's like he didn't *want* to stop the thief. This whole thing is bigger than we thought."

Rae raked her fingers through her hair. "You're definitely right about that."

Marcel and Martin Durand crossed the street and had nearly reached them. "I wonder how they happened to be here this morning just when the police were taking your uncle to jail," she whispered to her cousins.

"Let's see what we can find out," Cody said under his breath.

[Chapter Fourteen]

"Hi, Marcel. Hi, Monsieur Durand," Cody said. Otis and Rae gave a little wave. "You both saw what just happened."

Mr. Carson and Maxim came out of the house. They both nodded to Marcel and Monsieur Durand.

"We're going to the police station to speak with the director of police," said Maxim.

"Let us know if we can do anything to help," said Marcel, looking concerned. "I was just stopping by to see if you would have some free time to talk about painting with me, Mr. Carson—it would be such an honor. Of course, I see that now is not a good time."

"No, I'm sorry. Is there something we can do for you, Monsieur Durand?"

"*Non*, Monsieur Carson, I just happened to be in the neighborhood."

"Then we'll be on our way," Mr. Carson said. "I'll

call you later," he said to Rae and the twins. Then he and Maxim hurried toward the police station.

"Can one of you tell us what happened?" asked Marcel.

"I'm not sure where to begin," said Cody.

"It's all just so weird," Otis told them. "Detective Andrews had just walked out the door to go to work. All of a sudden we heard sirens. We looked out the window and saw a police car."

Cody told Marcel and Monsieur Durand everything that led up to the arrest. Otis and Rae added information.

"That's an outrage," fumed Monsieur Durand.

Otis noticed that he wasn't wearing the expensive Italian shoes that looked like the ones the thief had worn in the Louvre.

"I'd like to get my hands on that officer who insulted Detective Andrews," said Marcel.

"Terrible!" Monsieur Durand said. He looked down and frowned. He pulled a tissue from his pocket and wiped the front of his shiny black shoes. "That officer shouldn't treat anyone that way. And especially not a well-respected detective that he'd worked with!"

"You're not wearing your special Italian shoes," Otis noted. "Was the repair shop able to fix them for you after the cat scratched them up at the party the other night?"

Monsieur Durand threw his hands in the air. "I was on my way to pick them up from the repair shop when I saw Detective Andrews in the police car," he said. "I don't know why it took so long to fix them. I was beginning to suspect that the shop had lost them."

Otis swallowed. *Was Monsieur Durand telling the truth?* he wondered. *If so, that's one more suspect cleared.*

"My shoes aren't important right now," said Monsieur Durand. "We have to think of a way to get Detective Andrews out of jail and clear his name. You say you heard someone prowling around one night, and you think that person might have planted the paintings?"

"Yes," said Cody. "The paintings in the basement below my uncle's apartment were even easier to spot as forgeries than the ones placed in the galleries."

"The red in Van Gogh's beard in his self-portraits *is* hard to duplicate," said Marcel. "Of course, any great master painting is difficult to copy."

"I guess you'd know, since you paint copies of the great masters yourself," said Cody. "Um—has anyone suspicious ever commissioned a painting from you?" He studied Marcel's face as he waited for the answer. Inside, he was hoping that Marcel had nothing to do with the crimes.

Marcel's face reddened. Cody thought he looked flustered.

"Did I tell you about that little side business of mine?" Marcel asked.

"No," Cody admitted. "I happened to see your ad in the paper and recognized your phone number."

Marcel raised his eyebrows. "I paint the pictures for regular people," he said. "They love the paintings they see in galleries and museums but can't afford to own them. If I thought a client seemed suspicious, I wouldn't sell a painting to him." He cleared his throat. "I'd better be going now. If I think of anything that can help Detective Andrews, I'll give you a call."

"I'll be thinking, too," said Monsieur Durand. "*Au revoir* for now."

After Marcel and Monsieur Durand left, Rae and the twins went back inside to talk things over. They sat around the kitchen table, looking glum.

"I didn't like the way Marcel was acting," said Otis. "It definitely seemed like he had something to hide."

Rae let out a long sigh. "I know. I wish I didn't think so, but I do. We didn't even *mention* the Van Gogh portrait forgery. He brought up the red color in the beard on his own."

"Yes—but maybe he knew it was tough to copy because he'd tried it himself for a client," reasoned Otis. "I mean, maybe he brought it up without knowing the cops had found that particular picture."

Cody looked down. He was the most disappointed of all. "I guess we have to investigate Marcel," he said. He unfolded Marcel's ad that he'd been carrying in his pocket.

Otis asked to see it. "The ad includes the address 32 rue des Fleurs, #2B. Could be Marcel's apartment. I know you don't like the idea of snooping around behind Marcel's back, Cody, but I don't think we have a choice. Let's get this over with."

They had planned to hurry to the address in Marcel's ad. However, they found their feet dragging. Nobody wanted to suspect Marcel, much less break into his apartment. But if anything would help their uncle, they had to give it a try.

Thirty-two rue des Fleurs was not far from Chez Jules. On the way, they saw Jules coming out of the café and told him what had happened to their uncle.

"Under arrest? Framed? That's awful," Jules said. "The detective appears to be walking on *thin icing*." He raised his hand to his mouth. "I'm sorry, this is no time for jokes. I apologize. I'm sure that your uncle's innocence will be established."

"Thanks, Jules," said Cody. "We've got to get to the police station now," he fibbed.

"Good-bye, then, and good luck," Jules said.

They hurried to the building on rue des Fleurs. But when they got there, the outside door to the building was locked. Otis had brought along his lock-picking tools and wanted to go to work.

"Hang on a minute," Cody warned him. "There are lots of people passing by. I don't think we should be seen breaking into a building."

Otis crossed his arms. "Maybe so, but if we just hang around outside here, we're going to start attracting attention that way, too."

"Okay, okay, but let's just wait a minute."

Otis looked at Rae and rolled his eyes. She shrugged. "We can wait a little while. Check your watch and look up and down the street. People will think we're just waiting for someone."

"Okay." Otis looked at his watch and looked right and left, craning his neck. Then he looked at his watch again.

Meanwhile, Cody was worrying about the locks. He and Otis had learned to pick the locks by practicing on the doors at their house. They lived in the country, and it was a pain to get locked out when nobody was home. Then they got interested and friends let them practice on the locks at their houses. The skill had come in handy in detective work, but would he and Otis be able to handle unfamiliar French locks?

"I'm done waiting," said Otis impatiently. He bent down to examine the lock. Just then, a tiny gray-haired lady pushing a cart full of laundry opened the door. Otis jumped back. The woman eyed him strangely for a moment, then bustled away.

They all slipped inside and made their way up a flight of narrow old stairs. "There's 2B at the back," Otis said when they reached the landing. "It's the one with the boots by the door."

Otis took out his set of picks and started working on the lock. His hand shook. Often he could open modern locks with a library card. This lock was very old. "I think it takes a skeleton key," he whispered, poking around with a pick. He was about to give up when he heard a *click,* and the door opened. "*Whew,* let's do this," he said.

The apartment was small—just one room with a kitchen to one side and a tiny bathroom with the smallest sink they had ever seen. Most of the apartment was taken up by a table and an easel, and stacks of paintings and drawing pads. The one closet was barely big enough for a coat and a couple of shirts.

"There's a desk over here," said Rae. "I'll look through it, and you two can search the rest of the room." The three of them began picking through drawers and stacks of artwork, all the while listening for the sound of footsteps.

It didn't take long to find something. "This stack of paintings has a copy of every single one that's been stolen," Cody said regretfully. "There's more than one copy of some of the paintings. These forgeries are really, really good."

"Well, Marcel *told* us that he made copies of paintings," said Rae. "The ones that were stolen were well known, exactly the kind of paintings that people would hire someone to make legal copies of."

Cody let out a long sigh. "I hope that's all there is to it."

Rae and Otis looked at each other. "I'm sorry about Marcel, Cody," Otis said. "I like him, too. But he's definitely a suspect here."

Cody held out his hand in front of him as if he were going to push Otis away. "I know that, Otis. All I'm saying is that we don't have all the facts yet. Maybe he's an innocent guy just embarrassed about painting copies instead of his own stuff, so—" He stopped talking and cocked his head to one side. "Shh! I hear something."

There was the sound of heavy footsteps coming up the stairs. Cody and Otis prepared to dive under the bed. They motioned for Rae to join them, but then their hearts jumped into their throats. The bed rested on a platform with drawers. There was no under-the-bed space to hide in!

The closet was much too small to hold even one of them. The footsteps had reached the landing and were thudding toward the door. They had to get out of there right now.

The door opened and two men entered. They were each talking in loud, wise-guy voices. The twins had heard that kind of talk before, in movies full of crooks and wannabe crooks—these guys were definitely Americans.

Cody, Otis, and Rae crouched silently on the fire escape outside the small window. They had scrambled out there as the door opened, closing the window just in time. Now they all prayed that neither of the men decided to walk over and look at the view.

Marcel's apartment was at the back of the building. From the fire escape, they could see two blue-and-white vans parked on a side street. Both vans were painted with the Argent logo—a swirly silver "A."

"This Marcel guy is really talented, Manny," said a man with a gravelly voice.

"Yeah, lucky for us, Bubba!" Manny laughed—a long, high-pitched hyena cackle. "Come on, let's move it. Pick all those up. You can leave that one over there. Let's go. We can dump these babies in the back of the van and take a nice, long lunch."

Rae and the twins heard them clomping out. Then there was the sound of the door closing.

"We're going to have to get to that van and find out where they're going," Otis said as he and the others crawled back into the apartment. He peered out the window. "They're putting the paintings in one of the vans now. We can sneak in when they go to eat."

Cody spotted a painting leaning up against the wall with the back facing out. "I wonder why they left this one," he said. He turned the painting around and groaned. "Oh, no, look at this, you guys."

When Otis saw the painting, he scowled angrily. "That's *Birds in Flight*. Marcel took Dad's painting!"

[Chapter Fifteen]

"Are you sure that's not a fake?" Cody asked. "Why would they take the other paintings and leave that one here?"

"Good question," said Rae.

"Let's take a closer look at it," said Otis. He glanced out the window. "Bubba and Manny just loaded the paintings into the van and they're walking away. We have a little time."

Otis, Cody, and Rae lined themselves up in front of the painting and examined it carefully.

Cody was the one to break the silence. "It's a fake. Look at the color of that bird. In the real painting, it's bluer," he said decidedly.

"You're right," said Otis.

"Definitely," said Rae. She thought for a moment. "If Marcel paints the forgeries, why bring him one?"

Cody stroked his chin. "It could be that they're

trying to frame Marcel by planting evidence, the same way they're trying to frame Uncle Newton."

"Right!" Otis said. "It will look like he made the forgery of Dad's painting, and the others, too."

Rae was nodding. "Meanwhile, they can sell your dad's painting, keep all the money, and make someone else look guilty. I think it's just rotten, and—"

"Hold that thought," said Cody, peeking out the window once more. "We'd better get to the van." He began walking to the door, and then stopped in his tracks. *The van. Argent.*

Cody whirled around. "That small gallery owner—Claude—told us that he used Argent Contracting Company to fix his broken window, remember? And I'm almost positive he said that the other gallery owners always use that company, too, because they're so trustworthy. I think I even saw a couple of Argent vans near the Musée d'Orsay the day that weird portrait of Uncle Newton showed up."

Rae put her hands on her hips. "You're right! That museum was having some plaster repaired. And there were workmen all over the Louvre the afternoon we checked it out, too!"

"You don't have to paint *me* a picture. I get it," said Otis, nodding. "Those jerks had a pretty good game going. Thugs paid by Argent would break a window, and then the company would send someone in to scope out the place while they fixed what was broken. The perfect way to figure out how to steal something and not be suspected."

"They could have done some tampering while they were in the gallery, too," said Cody.

"What a setup," said Rae. "Argent must be a big outfit. I wonder if only one or two employees are crooked, or if the owner is involved."

"Let's think about it some more while we hitch a ride. We'd better get to that van."

The three of them crept down the stairs. They made sure the coast was clear before heading to the van.

"These guys are losers! They didn't even lock the door on the van," Otis said when he turned the handle. "Come on, hurry."

They all scrambled into the back of the first van they came to—the one they had watched Bubba and Manny load the paintings into. There wasn't much space because it was packed with framed art and sculptures. They had to scrunch into the small area between pieces of artwork. It was hot and dusty inside, and the dust made Cody's eyes water. Soon his nose was running, and then he started to sneeze. "*Achoo! Achoo!*"

"Cody, cut it out!" Otis said sharply. "We've gotta be quiet!"

"I'm not *trying* to sneeze," Cody said defensively. "It's just really dusty in here! *Achoo!*"

"Use your sleeve like a filter and breathe through that," suggested Rae. "If you give us away, we're in triple trouble."

They stopped talking as the front door of the van opened. A driver got in and slammed it shut. The engine started, and they were on their way. At first they didn't know if the driver of their van was Manny or Bubba. Soon they knew it was Manny. He liked to talk a lot and was constantly placing and receiving cell phone calls. They listened closely for information.

"Hey, it's Manny. Yep, everything went real smooth. What d'ya mean, slow? We were in and out. We loaded the stuff, and I'm on the road right now. *Ha-ha-ha!* You can say that again! Soon we'll be *rollin' in dough* and your pals will be left holding the bag." His laughter sounded forced. Manny paused, listening to whoever was on the other end of the call. "You're a funny guy, ya know that? I gotta tell Bubba that one: gettin' Andrews arrested was *the icing on the cake. Ha ha!* Okay, okay, I'll pay attention to the road. I'm hangin' up now."

Manny snorted and began muttering to himself.

"Jerk. Who does he think he is, telling me to get off the phone? He thinks he's better than I am. That detective and his artsy friends don't know him like I do. He's a big, sneaky French snake."

Manny kept snorting and muttering under his breath. He started bragging about how much smarter he was than "the big guy." By the time the van pulled to a stop, Rae and the twins were thinking Manny was a real wacko.

Manny was all smiles when he parked the van, slid down from the driver's seat, and called, "Hello, Monsieur Argent!"

Cody peered out the back window of the van. Argent Contracting Company was a rambling one-story building with few windows. Its worn bricks were a drab gray, but the silver "A" logo had been freshly painted on the metal doors. Cody shifted his gaze to the right and saw Manny talking to a very short, wiry man with steel-gray hair. It didn't make sense that Manny would call *him* the "big guy." He was definitely *not* big. *Who had Manny been talking to on the phone?* wondered Cody.

"Wait till you see all the stuff we have in the van for you," Manny said. "You won't be sorry you hired me and Bubba."

Monsieur Argent rubbed his hands together and

smiled. "I'll admit that I was against the idea at first. But when I heard about the jobs you'd pulled and I thought about the money, I was convinced."

Rae, Cody, and Otis ducked down below the back window of the van and froze in place. They could hear Manny and Monsieur Argent getting closer and closer. The handle on the back door of the van tilted down, and the door began to open. Then a voice called out, "Hey, don't unpack that stuff yet. Come on in and take a load off for a while. There's plenty of work to do, and you'll need to rest up."

The door shut and the footsteps headed toward the front of the van. Rae and the twins heard one of the front doors being opened and shut, and breathed out sighs of relief.

"I've got it," Manny said.

"What's he carrying?" Otis whispered.

Cody craned his neck, but from his vantage point out the back window, Manny was hidden from view.

"Whatever it is, they must be taking it inside," said Cody. "We've got to get out of here and find a back way into the warehouse. Then we can poke around and hear what they talk about."

The three of them crept out of the van. They kept an eye out for people as they hurried to the rear of the warehouse building.

The first two doors they tried were locked. "There's *no jamb we can't handle!*" Otis whispered. He grinned as he wrenched open the third door. With their hearts hammering, Rae and the twins eased their way inside. With every step, they watched for the slightest movement and listened for the faintest sound.

They hurried down a long hallway with rooms on either side. The rooms were loaded with tools, paint, sand, bricks, glass, and other building materials. Then the twins and Rae came to a larger room.

There were a few stacks of paintings and sculptures, along with some other valuables, such as antique vases and lamps, chairs, and rugs. "This operation is really, really big," Rae whispered in awe.

"It certainly is," Cody said in a hushed voice. "I think we're in over our heads. It would take a whole organization to deal with this much stuff, not just one or two goofy crooks like Manny and Bubba."

"I'm calling the police." Otis whipped out his cell phone. He started punching in numbers.

Cody grabbed his hand. "What if you end up talking to an officer who's really one of the crooks? Think about the one who insulted Uncle Newton."

Otis shook his head. "That guy was working in the field, not answering phones. We need help."

Just then they heard a groan coming from a corner of the room. They heard it again and followed the sound to a row of statues. They tiptoed around them and saw a man tied to a chair. His head was bent forward, his chin on his chest. His dark hair was matted with blood, and there were little spots of blood on his shirt.

Cody went over and crouched down so he could look into the man's face. It was Marcel! He looked as if he'd been badly beaten. His cheek was cut and bruised, and one eye was swollen shut. He'd been knocked out, but now one eyelid began to flutter. When he recognized Cody, he straightened up abruptly.

Marcel tried to say something, but he only made thick, slurred sounds. Cody started to untie him, but Marcel began to shake his head back and forth. His eyes were wild. "Get out of here, now!" He managed to force the whisper through his lips.

"What happened to you? Why did they beat you?" Cody asked. He kept trying to untie Marcel's bindings.

"Stop!" Marcel hissed. "We're dealing with vicious criminals here, and if they find you, you're in serious trouble."

"But you've been working with them, haven't you?" Cody asked. "It looks like they turned on you."

Marcel gritted his teeth. "There's no time to

explain. I can deal with these guys, but you have to get out of here right now. If they catch you, you can't help me. Then I'm done for, and so is Detective Andrews."

Marcel ran his tongue over his dry, cracked lips. "Listen to me, all of you," he said. "Behind those stacks of paintings over there is a way to get to a secret elevator. Open the lid of the big antique trunk. You'll see that the bottom has been cut out to hide a hole in the floor. Climb down the ladder to the platform. The elevator is right there."

He paused and licked his lips again. He looked terribly thirsty. "There are some miner's caps in the elevator. Make sure the ones you take light up. I hope you brought some flashlights."

Cody nodded quickly.

"Good. Hold onto them," rasped Marcel. "Take the elevator all the way down. When you get out, you'll find some tracks. Follow those tracks, no matter what. It's easy to get lost. The tracks will lead you to another elevator. Manny and his goons installed two down there. The numbers are on the doors. Take elevator number two up to the street, then run for the police."

Questions formed in Cody's mind. *How far away was the second elevator? What if the manhole was blocked? What if the elevator didn't work? What would the bad guys do to Marcel?*

The sound of voices laughing and talking reached Rae and the twins. There were grunts and thuds as the vans were unloaded. Footsteps were headed closer.

Just as two men entered the large room, Cody, Otis, and Rae hurried behind the stacks of paintings and crouched down. They saw the trunk that Marcel told them would lead to the elevator. It was too late to get inside, but at least they could hear what was going on from their hiding place. One of the men started talking in French.

"Ya gotta speak English, boss," Manny said in a jokey voice. "My French is . . . how do you say? *Zero.*"

"All right. I'll speak slowly, too."

There was a nasty laugh, and the speaker continued, this time addressing Marcel. "The joke is on you, art genius. When the real cops find the forgery of Carson's painting in your apartment, you're going to jail along with your detective pal and Manny's old prison buddy with the fancy-schmancy shoes, who thinks he's such a straight arrow now. Seeing all of you bundled off to prison will be like *having my cake and eating it, too.*"

Cody bit his lip. His mind started whirling, and things started falling into place. He suddenly knew who had set up Uncle Newton, and who was now gloating over his arrest. It had been Jules, the café owner, all along.

[Chapter Sixteen]

Manny laughed, a strange combination of a cackle and a howl. "That's real funny, Jules," he said. "You make cakes, and then you *have your cake and eat it, too.*"

"Why do you always repeat my jokes, idiot?" Jules snapped. Then he turned to Marcel again. "It's too bad you started getting nosy and figuring things out. Then you started talking to your despicable friend Detective Andrews."

"I created those paintings you hung on the walls of your restaurant for free, Jules," Marcel said. "You used me."

"Yes, yes, you were very useful, and you never suspected what I was really up to. I kept giving you assignments from my 'friends.' I handed you the money you thought came from them. You were so much better than the other forgers we had used! We were able to sell your paintings as originals!"

"You're disgusting."

The sound of a slap cracked through the air. "Shaddup!" said Manny. "Don't talk to Jules that way."

"No more violence, please. It's so crude," said Jules. "I'm sorry that Manny and Bubba beat you up, Marcel—I didn't mean for that to happen. All I care about is the *dough*."

Manny snickered.

"I'll let you in on a little secret, Marcel," Jules continued. "Here's how I planned to frame the *framer,* too. I hate Durand, the way he acts like the detective's puppy dog. He's always talking about how *fantastique* he is. The detective sent him to prison! What's so *fantastique* about that?" Jules snorted.

Jules chuckled. "It's a funny story, actually. I went to pick up a pair of my shoes from Lamont's repair shop the day I tried to rob the Louvre. It was very busy in the shop that day, and they gave me Monsieur Durand's shoes by mistake. I couldn't believe my luck. I thought I might leave one in the museum as evidence for the guards to find—that would have gotten rid of the little dog. But when I tried on the shoes, they were so comfortable that I ended up wearing them that night instead." Jules paused and smiled.

What a heel, Otis punned to himself, thinking about how Jules had set up not only Marcel and Uncle Newton but also Monsieur Durand.

"I had to go to the trouble of planting a real painting in Durand's apartment," continued Jules, "just to be sure he got blamed as an accomplice, too. The police will be convinced that you are *both* working with Detective Andrews. *Oh là là!* I'm *on a roll!*"

Cody and Otis looked at each other anxiously. They both had asked themselves why Jules was telling Marcel so much about his crimes. They had come up with the same answer: Jules wasn't really planning to turn Marcel over to the police at all. He was telling him everything because he didn't think Marcel would last long enough to tell anybody else.

"Come on, Manny, let's get going," said Jules. "There's lots of work to do tonight. We'll figure out how to feed you to the police later, Marcel."

"How about the special package, boss?" Manny asked. "The fifty thousand dollars?"

"Patience, Manny, patience!" snapped Jules.

As they began walking away, Marcel called out, "Wait! I just want to know one more thing. Why are you so angry with the detective, anyway?"

"Surely you know, *non*? I had a wonderful chef, and business at the café was booming. Then Detective Andrews sent him to jail for some *little trifle* of a crime. He stole a few drawings that weren't worth much."

"You told me he was making counterfeit money," Manny blurted out. "That's a pretty *big* crime."

"Idiot! Who asked you?" Jules shouted. "Let's go."

When Marcel was sure Manny and Jules were far enough away, he called for Rae and the twins to come out. "I just thought of something," he said. "All of this art is here because they're packing it up and sending it out tonight. Usually everything is kept in an underground vault. You'll see when you take the elevator." He coughed and grimaced in pain.

"They're going to be bringing up more pieces," he continued. "If the elevator isn't here when they want it, they'll know someone else has used it. They'll definitely be suspicious and start looking around. As soon as you get off the elevator, send it right back up as fast as you can. Now, go! Go!"

Without another word, the three kids climbed into the trunk one by one. They found the ladder that led to the elevator and began climbing down as fast as they dared. They reached a platform that faced an elevator. They pushed the button, opened the door, and climbed in.

The elevator began descending into the catacombs. They picked up miner's caps from a pile in the corner and tested them before putting them on. "There aren't any floors so we can't tell how much farther we have to go," Rae said tensely. "This thing is slow!"

Otis tapped his foot. "Come on, come on, hurry up," he muttered. "Hey, Cody, you didn't look surprised when you heard Jules was the main thief."

"Remember how Jules always made puns about desserts? They were almost as corny as yours, Otis! When I heard the guy in the warehouse making more terrible puns, everything started to fit together."

Otis was scowling. "He pretended to be our friend—and Uncle Newton's friend, too. And my puns are a *whole* lot better than his."

"Not sure about that," said Rae. "But you're right about him being a nasty traitor."

The elevator gave a little bounce and then stopped. The doors opened, and Rae pressed the button to send the elevator up before they dashed out. "That must be where they leave the stolen art before they transport it to the crooked buyer!" Otis pointed to a huge container that looked like a bank vault.

"It's gigantic," said Rae. "It must have taken forever to get the parts down here."

"That's why it was important to have Monsieur Argent on their side," said Cody. "They needed a big building like his warehouse. Over there are the tracks Marcel told us about."

They saw three metal bins on wheels sitting near the vault. "I guess they use those to wheel the art down the tracks to the vault," said Otis. "A thief could steal something and disappear down a manhole anywhere in Paris, and then find his way here to stash the art."

"Hey! That's how those guys who broke Claude's window disappeared so fast!" said Cody, snapping his fingers.

"C'mon, let's move," Rae urged.

They all began jogging down the track. The little headlamps on their caps illuminated only a few feet in front of them. They could make out the ancient tunnel walls on either side and not much else. This wasn't a fun trip, like the one they'd had with Marcel. There was no laughing and joking, and no party to look forward to. Their thoughts turned darker.

How many bones from how many skeletons were there with them? Were there cataphiles who had gone down there alive and never seen daylight again? It would be pretty easy to get lost. As much as they told themselves it was silly, they couldn't stop thinking of hauntings.

The tracks swerved to the right, and the tunnel began to slope downward. They were all breathing heavily. Little by little, they slowed their pace until they were walking.

Rae felt something soft—like the webbed feet of a duck—brush her neck. She heard a rustling sound as claws grazed her hair, and she let out a high, thin shriek. "Bats!"

Suddenly, Rae, Cody, and Otis were surrounded by bats, filling the air with the *whoosh!* of their wings. Rae and the twins flailed their arms wildly over their heads as they ran. They felt the brush of wings and the prickle of claws on their arms, on their legs, in their hair, and on their faces. Soon they were all screaming as they ran along the tracks.

Then the bats were gone as suddenly as they had appeared. The twins and Rae slowed to catch their breath. It took a while before they could stop brushing their hands over their bodies, as if the bats were still there.

"I guess the bats didn't scare *you*, Rae," Otis said teasingly. He let out an imitation of her shriek.

"It sounded like they were driving you a little *batty*." Cody laughed.

"Cut it out," she said angrily. "You two weren't

exactly fearless." She turned her head. "Do you hear that? I hear something rattling."

Cody and Otis froze in terror. The darkness, the tunnels, the *rattling*. Their minds flared with images from their nightmares.

They listened intently to the rattling, which had been joined by a steady *ca-ching, ca-ching, ca-ching*. It was getting louder by the second. They all realized at the same time what was making the sound.

"It's the wheels on one of those bins. They're after us!" Cody said. "Hurry!"

They all began running as fast as they could go. Behind them, the ominous rattling sound kept getting louder and louder . . . and closer and closer. Manny's eerie, hyena-like laughter tore through the darkness as he cackled madly.

[Chapter Seventeen]

"We can't outrun that cart—it's coming too fast!" Cody cried. "We've got to get off the tracks before it catches up to us!"

As frightening as it was to think about getting lost in the endless tunnels, they all knew they had no choice but to run into the unknown darkness. They would have to memorize every turn and every marker so they could find their way back to the tracks again later.

A tunnel headed left, and they took it. Now they were heading deep underground without a compass. The catacombs closed around them.

The three kept up a steady pace through the tunnel. "Let's stick with this one," Rae called as other tunnels began branching off. Behind them in the distance, they heard the bin go rolling past the place where they had turned off the tracks.

"I have to stop for a minute," Otis panted. Like his brother and his cousin, he was breathing in desperate, ragged gasps. "I think it's safe to go back to the tracks," he said when he could speak.

Something quickly changed his mind: Manny the Mole's crazy laugh erupted and echoed through the tunnels. "Did you kids think we couldn't see you down here? We have cameras *everywhere!*"

"Run!" Otis yelled. The others were already racing ahead. Soon he couldn't see them anymore. Just like in his nightmare, Otis was being chased through a tunnel of bones. *I'd give anything to wake up right now*, he said to himself. Manny was closing in on him, his footsteps pounding relentlessly. Ahead was a hill of bones. Otis almost stumbled into it, but stopped short just in time. He dashed into a tunnel to his right.

Otis ran through an open area where cataphiles had created an underground club. Tiled walls, tables and chairs, and a stage flashed past his eyes. Further along, he ran through what looked like an ancient underground shelter. There were toilets caked with dirt and old sinks on the ground. The tunnel kept widening.

He kept running, but he soon felt Manny's hot breath on his neck. Then he felt the man's thick arm around his neck and chest, pulling him to a stop. "I've got you now, you meddling little cockroach," Manny snarled and cackled in his ear.

If there was ever a time to use my karate skills, thought Otis, *this is it*. He slammed his boot on Manny's instep. Then he elbowed him in the ribs. Manny let go with a cry of surprise. Then Otis did what his sensei had always told him to do if he was ever under attack: *run*.

Otis raced on, hearing the thud of Manny's feet behind him. In some part of his brain, Otis was relieved that he had only one pursuer—and that it was *human*, not a walking, talking skeleton.

Suddenly, Otis felt something dash over his foot. It was much too large to be a mouse. *Rats!* thought Otis. Another one scurried by—Otis could hear its sharp claws skittering over the floor of the tunnel. Another one dropped from the ceiling and landed on his shoulder. He brushed it away with a huge shudder of disgust.

Something else landed on his shoulder. It was Manny's hand. Manny whirled him around. His face was wild with rage. "Why, you little . . . I'll finish you right now!"

Otis kicked Manny in the kneecap as hard as he could. Manny let out a cry of pain and fury as Otis squirmed away and ran.

"Stop!" Manny yelled. Otis brushed against the wall. Skulls that had been stacked carefully began tumbling to the floor. Then the whole wall crashed down in a cascade of skulls and bones. Otis crunched over them as he brushed off the rats that kept falling on him. Behind him, Manny began to scream, "Help me! The rats! The rats! Get them off me!"

Otis's lungs were on fire. He stopped, breathing heavily, and turned on his flashlight. He shone the beam all around. What he saw made his insides crackle with fear. Hundreds of skulls grinned from the pile, and stacked bones still decorated parts of the walls. But what made the scene a million times more gruesome was that rats were everywhere. They balanced on thigh bones and pushed their faces through empty eye sockets and between crooked teeth. They swarmed around Otis's feet and all over the pile of bones in a gigantic, moving rat carpet. Otis was too stunned by the sight to be sick, almost too horrified to move. *They're just animals*, he reminded himself. Inside, something clicked. He'd always had a special, almost magical connection with animals. It had saved him in other situations, and he felt suddenly sure that he could use it to help him in this one.

He began to look around at the rats, calmly and

slowly. Wordlessly, he began communicating with the swarming mass of creatures. After a few moments, they all stopped moving and looked up at him with their bright eyes. One by one, they began to move away from him, retreating back through the wall of bones. But they continued to scurry over Manny, who alternated between screaming in fear and laughing wildly. "I'm afraaaid!" he wailed.

Suddenly, Otis remembered something that Maxim had read in the newspaper article about Manny the Mole: he had a serious case of *musophobia*, an uncontrollable fear of rats. Otis figured that Manny was more afraid of the rats than Otis was of Manny. And even though Manny was a rotten guy, Otis knew he couldn't leave him down in the catacombs alone to die of fright—or to be eaten alive by rodents with sharp yellow teeth.

"Manny, we're going to start walking," he called. "I'll be right behind you. Stay with me, and I won't let anything happen to you."

"P-p-promise?" Manny blubbered. His terror of rats had turned him from a frightening gangster into a frightened child.

"I promise," Otis said. "But you have to do *exactly* what I tell you to. Put your hands behind your back."

Otis took off his belt and tied Manny's hands together with it. "Okay, let's go."

As he walked, Otis kept calling out for Cody and Rae. He forced himself to keep calm. He found the tracks and the abandoned cart, and soon a call answered his own. "Over here, Otis!" He recognized his brother's voice and hurried toward it.

Cody and Rae ran toward him. "What happened to you—where'd you go?" They stopped and stared at Manny, who was shaking all over.

"The guy's *really* afraid of rats," Otis explained. "There's a million of them back there."

They walked to elevator number two, as Marcel had told them to, and Cody punched the "up" button. After a lengthy pause, the elevator doors opened.

"Go ahead, Manny, get in," said Otis.

Manny stopped babbling for a moment. He looked at Otis with wide, frightened eyes. "Rats? Rats?"

"No, Manny, there are no rats in the elevator," Otis said calmly. "It will take you away from the rats."

Manny went into the elevator quietly. Rae and the twins followed, slumping against the walls in exhaustion. The elevator began carrying them out of the catacombs and back to the surface.

The elevator doors opened, revealing a long ladder.

Otis took the lead and began climbing. People gawked as the foursome emerged from a hole in the street. When they were all safely out, Otis pushed the manhole cover back in place while Cody hailed a police car. One of the officers got on the radio, and things started happening very fast.

Within seconds, an ambulance arrived and whisked the hysterical Manny to a hospital. As he was being loaded onto the gurney, he let out one of his crazy laughs and babbled on about rats.

Thanks to the efforts of Maxim and Mr. Carson, Detective Andrews had been released from jail earlier in the evening. And just as soon as the twins and Rae breathlessly told him what they had discovered, he ordered a team of officers he trusted to fan out and make arrests around the city. The late-night crowd at Chez Jules was shocked when two policemen led Jules out of the restaurant in handcuffs. There was a panic at the Argent headquarters when officers surrounded the place. Monsieur Argent tried to escape into the catacombs, but one of the policemen caught him as he climbed down the hidden ladder under the warehouse trunk.

Detective Andrews, accompanied by his trusted police team and a gaggle of fascinated news reporters and photographers, opened the vault underneath the catacombs. The detective had expected to find priceless masterpieces, but the amount of stolen art was truly amazing. The photographers stared in shock at the piles of paintings and rows of statues before they started snapping photos. The reporters tripped over each other trying to get the first interview with the heroic detective who had broken the case. Detective Andrews smiled and posed for photo after photo with Cody, Otis, and Rae. He gave them full credit for helping him bust the ring of art thieves.

When the stolen items were examined, they totaled more than a billion dollars. In the weeks that followed, most of the items that had been shipped out were also recovered.

[Chapter Eighteen]

Maxim stretched out his legs, leaned back in his chair, and looked around the den. Then he folded his newspaper carefully and put it on the coffee table. "Ah, back home in Deerville, where nothing crazy ever happens. It's so relaxing."

Mr. Carson sat on the sofa, with his computer on his lap. "Listen to this: It's an e-mail from Newton. It's quite an update! There has been a shake-up at the police department. He's been given a formal apology."

"He should have gotten one the day he was released," said Rae.

"You're right about that, Rae," said Mr. Carson. He raised his eyebrows. "He writes here that the Paris police director was arrested for accepting bribes from Monsieur Argent. That explains why the director kept Newton busy with stolen cameo brooches and missing dogs for so long! The officer who insulted him was found to be crooked, too."

"He *did* seem more like a crook than a police officer," said Otis.

Mr. Carson went back to reading the e-mail. "Both of them had ties to an international organization of art thieves. Jules had been part of it for years."

"What will happen to Chez Jules now?" Maxim asked.

Mr. Carson smiled. "Newton says the chef and his wife will buy it. The chef is a very nice young man, and he makes all of the pastries himself."

"He is very talented." Cody sighed and rubbed his belly. "He deserves to have his own restaurant!" He was quiet for a moment. "Why do you think Jules became a criminal in the first place?"

Mr. Carson sighed. "I guess he was angry, and he wanted money. Somehow he got mixed up with crooks who told him crime would be an easy way to grab it. Of course, he thought he would keep getting away with it. Thanks to you three, his life of crime was cut short. You should be very proud of how many paintings you saved."

"We *did* see some pretty great paintings while we were in Paris," Cody said, his eyes twinkling. "Rae told me that her favorites were Degas' ballet dancers. Of course, *Degas aged*. That's a pretty good palindrome, don't you think?"

Otis rolled his eyes. "I don't know. How old was Degas when he died?"

Mr. Carson clicked his laptop lid closed. "Edgar Degas lived to be eighty-three years old. You're quite right, Cody—clever palindrome."

"Superb," said Maxim. He yawned and leaned down to pat Dude, the dog, on the head. Dude was napping, but his tail wagged once.

Cody smiled triumphantly.

Otis poked his brother in the ribs. "Two can play at that game," he said. "How about a killer pun for you? Degas had *a brush with greatness*."

"Nice one!" said Cody, poking him back.

"You two are the weirdest cousins in the universe," said Rae in exasperation. Then she shrugged and allowed herself a smile. She thought, *If you can't beat 'em, join 'em*.

"Hey, guys: What did the art thief say to the crooked art collector?" Rae's dark eyes twinkled. When neither twin could answer, she burst out, "*Show me the Monet!*"

As her cousins collapsed into laughter, Rae began to imagine their next vacation together. She already knew it wouldn't be relaxing, but it also *definitely* wouldn't be boring!